DANCE WITH THE DEVIL

by

Geoff Collins

This book is a work of fiction. Names, characters, places and incidents are either the product of the author's imagination or are used fictitiously. Any resemblance to actual persons, living or dead, or to actual events or locales is entirely coincidental.

DANCE WITH THE DEVIL

Front/Back cover designed by: Telemachus Press
Front cover art: ID 66336650 StokketeDreamstime.com
Back cover art: Bullets Pixabay
Interior art: Dog illustration: Pixabay

Edited by Joe Gartrell and Ben Gibson of Word Mule. www.wordmule.com

Published by A&J Publishing, LLC
3266 Hartwell Street
Johns Island, SC 29455

Visit the author's website: www.booksbycollins.com

Categories: FICTION/Thrillers Crime

ISBN: 978-1-956867-25-1 (eBook)
ISBN: 978-1-956867-24-4 (paperback)

Version: 2022.03.16

www.projectpawsalive.org

A special thanks to Joe Gartrell and Ben Gibson of Word Mule.
www.wordmule.com

This book is dedicated to …

My Wonderful Family

BOOKS BY GEOFF COLLINS

"A Holy City Mystery Artfully Spun"

"Geoff Collins is a wonderfully versatile writer (check out his bibliography), and here, he weaves a delightful mystery set in the Holy City. Hop along and crack this case with Giordano—you won't regret, and it will get you primed for the other books coming along in the series."

"Well Written … Interesting Characters and Plenty of Suspense"

"Good mystery with interesting characters and plenty of suspense. A cybersecurity expert is hired to determine if narcotics theft is taking place at Charleston SC hospital and who is behind it. Well written with lots of fascinating details."

"Wonderfully Crafted Story Set in Charleston"

"Wonderfully crafted story set in Charleston, SC—great story line and vivid imagery. Collins follows Giordano with insight and honesty. Can't wait for Nick's next adventure."

"A Fast and Exciting Read"

"The book was a fast read. It was exciting and held my interest throughout. Hope to see more from this author."

"Another Wild Ride"

"Tools of the Trade takes us on another wild ride with Nick Giordano and his crew. Collins, as he did with his previous book in this three-part series, deftly weaves on intricate story line that builds to a satisfying, thrilling end. Highly recommend Collins, a writer who deserves a vast readership."

"Excitement and Suspense"

"Excitement and suspense as mafia and white supremacists fight over the drug market in Charleston SC. Characters well-developed and interesting story line."

"Hopefully More to Come"

"In this series, which sadly wraps here with Book Three, Collins found a higher gear with each, serving up a fresh batch of nasty folks for the series' core characters to root out and take down. That the books were set in Charleston only added to their delight. The only rotten aspect here is that this is the last we'll see of Nick Giordano and his pals—that is, unless, this crew comes around for cameos in one of Collins' future works. Hats off!"

*"You can get much further with a kind word and a gun
than you can with a kind word alone."*

—Al Capone

*"Never quit. Never surrender. Never fail. Adapt to the
situation. Gain and maintain the initiative."*

—The Marine Raiders—Spiritus Invictus

Dance with the Devil

PROLOGUE

THE GRAY-HAIRED MAN sat patiently behind the wheel of a brown Honda Civic in the darkened parking lot of the Black Diamond Club. The time was half-past two in the morning, and only two other cars remained in the strip club's lot. A steady drizzle had fallen over the last few hours, leaving the pot-holed lot spotted with shimmering pools of rainwater. The gray-haired man was clothed in baggy corduroy pants, a pair of old partially laced work boots, and a soiled T-shirt under an oversized tattered army jacket. He pulled his threadbare ballcap lower over his forehead and checked that his sham beard remained firmly in place. Before exiting the Honda, the last thing he did was slip on a pair of black surgical gloves.

He moved away from the Honda to a position about fifteen feet from a late model red Chevy Camaro and waited in the shadows. The night breeze had picked up a bit, and the dim light from the spotlights on the club filtered through the branches of the trees that lined the building—dragging ghostly shapes across the nearly vacant parking lot. Except for the club's red neon sign, the sky was painted shades of thunder-cloud gray. The night was tranquil, broken only by an intermittent rumble of distant thunder and the continuous patter of rain against the wet pavement.

Cornell Jackson stepped out of the bar and paused for a moment under the glow of the club's neon sign. He glanced up at a dark night sky and pulled up the collar of his old blue and white Los Angeles Dodgers jacket. He moved quickly to his Camaro, but before reaching the car, he noticed what looked like a homeless man heading unsteadily toward him.

"Hey, buddy," the man mumbled, "you got a couple bucks I can borrow?"

"Fuck off," Jackson said and pulled out his car keys.

Cornell Jackson never saw the flash from the taser or heard the audible click as the compressed nitrogen cylinders exploded, firing two barbs directly through his jacket, embedding themselves in his chest. The wires attached to the barbs carried 1,200 volts of electricity—sending his muscles into violent, sustained contractions. Jackson was on the ground, totally incapacitated and writhing in pain a second later.

The gray-haired man removed a hypodermic needle from the pocket of his army jacket and carefully uncapped it. Dripping with propofol, he plunged it deep into Jackson's neck, emptying the entire contents of the syringe—immediately rendering him unconscious. Jackson was dragged behind the Honda and quickly deposited in the car's trunk. Thirty seconds later, the gray-haired man exited the Black Diamond's parking lot and had the Honda on its way out of Charleston.

CHAPTER 1

ALESSIO MESSINA STOOD motionless against the wall in the back room of Callaghan's Bar. He worked for Frank Romano, the head of the Organization's operations in Charleston.

Alessio's eyes were riveted on the bar's owner, Michael Coppola, who sat behind the desk in the back room—a room Coppola considered his office. His "office" looked like a storage room with brown cardboard liquor boxes stacked high against one wall. The kind of metal shelving commonly found in warehouses lined the opposing wall and held cases of beer and various bar cleaning supplies. Coppola had several framed photos of himself during his trips to Italy, and a few garish Italian travel posters hung on the wall behind his desk. Callaghan's Bar was located on Dorchester Road in North Charleston, and his associates took great pleasure in reminding Coppola how peculiar it was that he was Italian and worked out of the back of an Irish bar.

Michael Coppola was a bull of a man. An avid weightlifter when he was younger, he'd lost interest over the years, and it was clear that good food and drink had gotten the upper hand. His receding hair was combed straight back; his pants belted a bit too high above his waist.

A hint of a smile appeared on Coppola's face as he disconnected his cell phone and nodded to Messina. His attention shifted to the gray-haired man sitting directly across from him. The man seemed frail, almost effeminate—except for his eyes—dark and menacing eyes as if a soul once resided there but had long since departed. The gray-haired man was unique in his chosen profession. Growing up in the theater with his dramatically alcoholic, mediocre actress of a mother, he became adept with using makeup and disguises—creating various characters to escape his chaotic upbringing. His late teens and twenties brought an infatuation with all forms of weapons, especially knives.

Coppola leaned forward and smiled. "The rest of your money has been deposited as you instructed. Are you sure this was a clean job? No loose ends, as they say."

The gray-haired man returned Coppola's stare for an uncomfortable moment before saying, "I'm not in a business that tolerates loose ends, Mr. Coppola. The individual you desired eliminated has been. It was clean. No loose ends, as they say."

The gray-haired man had met Coppola only once before and disliked him immediately. This was unusual. He'd always divorced himself from any emotional reaction to his clients or why they required his services. Emotion could be deadly in his line of work. The gray-haired man knew Coppola's operation played a relatively minor part within the Organization, and under normal circumstances, he would never have even entertained a contract from the man. However, Alessio Messina had advised the gray-haired man that Mr. Romano also expressed an interest in removing the target and made a recommendation he accept the contract—*recommendation* being the operative word.

The gray-haired man stood and removed a small plastic baggie from his pocket. There was a key inside the baggie, which he placed on the desk in front of Coppola.

"As agreed, you are to dispose of the vehicle."

"That will be taken care of," Coppola replied.

"Good, then we are done here."

The man stood and turned to leave but stopped when Coppola asked, "Where's the body?"

The comment confirmed the man's opinion of Coppola. "That is not your concern. It has been dealt with. I suggest you leave it at that."

The gray-haired man nodded at Alessio, and the two left together.

Coppola remained seated for another moment, congratulating himself for disposing of Cornell Jackson. He'd never been involved in murder for hire before, but he felt comfortable with it since his boss had also sanctioned the hit. He had no regrets taking out Jackson, who he considered a two-bit, punk-ass pissant. But this pissant and his teenage boys had been picking away at his drug business the past six months. Although his operation was relatively small, Coppola had always met his agreed-upon percentage to the Organization and kept his business within his boundaries. *I should have done it sooner*, he thought to himself.

He stood and left his second-floor office and entered the back of the bar—lit only by a fluorescent light hanging low over a well-worn pool table. He scanned the bar until he eyed Jimmy Sanborn, his bodyguard and confidant. To say Sanborn was a big man wouldn't come close to doing him justice. At 6'5" and 280, everything about the man was big—from his massive head to hands the size of bear claws to his size 15 ½ shoes. He'd grown up in the Brentwood neighborhood and had gained some level of notoriety as a club fighter. He was fiercely loyal to Michael Coppola—a loyalty finding its origin one night fifteen years ago when he was walking back to the room he rented on Lupine Street. He'd just left the Dorsey Road VFW Hall after winning a fierce ten-round fight with an Armenian when he was jumped by three men. They took him down with a tire iron to the back of his head. After a series of vicious punches and kicks, the thieves began rifling through his pockets.

At that moment, the night was shattered by three deafening gunshots fired from Michael Coppola's .38 Special echoing down the alleyway. The three muggers scattered. Coppola and two of his men managed to carry the semiconscious Sanborn back to Callaghan's, where they did their best to attend to his injuries. After a few weeks of recovering from the beating he took that night, Coppola offered him a job as one of his bodyguards. Jimmy Sanborn pledged his loyalty to Coppola from that time on, eventually becoming his boss' confidant and most trusted ally.

Coppola called out to Sanborn, and Jimmy made his way to the back of the bar.

"Who you got working tonight?" Coppola asked.

"Johnny and Vic are handling the girls," Sanborn answered.

"Who else you got?"

"The other boys are out collecting or at home."

"Anyone else," Coppola persisted.

"Not really. Well, the new kid, Eddie Russo, is here. What'd you need done?"

Eddie was a 22-year-old squirrelly-looking kid—definitely not the sharpest tool in the toolshed. But he seemed harmless. Eddie's dad, Pete Russo, had worked for Coppola since he started his operation back in the late 90s. However, about ten years ago, Pete Russo was killed in a car accident. Since his wife had split to parts unknown years before, his eleven-year-old son, Eddie, found himself living with his dad's sister, Martha Russo. Even though Martha was less than a stellar citizen, Michael made sure she had enough money to keep a roof over Eddie's head and put food on the table. Eddie had a few minor brushes with the law as a teenager but was recently charged and convicted of petty theft. He did 30 days in the Charleston Correctional Center and was fined $1,000—which Michael Coppola paid. To keep an eye on the boy, Michael allowed Eddie to hang around Callaghan's for the last month or so, running errands and doing odds and ends for the guys.

Coppola tossed Sanborn the baggie with the key in it. "There's a brown Honda Civic parked next to the bar. Tell the kid to take it out to Park's Auto Salvage in Goose Creek and make sure Gino gets it. I told Gino he's getting a car today. He knows what to do with it."

"How's Eddie going to get back?" Sanborn asked.

"Anyone else out there?" Coppola asked.

"Just Eddie and some of the old guys. You want I should call Johnny or Vic to come in?"

"No," Coppola said. "I need them working the whores. They'll steal us blind if nobody's watching them. I'll have one of Gino's guys at the salvage yard give him a ride back to his place."

"All right," Sanborn said, "I'll take care of it."

"One more thing, Jimmy," Coppola added. "Tell Eddie to keep his fucking mouth shut about this."

Sanborn got Eddie and told him to follow him to the parking lot, where he pointed out the brown Honda that was parked there.

The gray-haired man had just retrieved a small satchel from the Honda and was getting into the front seat of Alessio's Dodge Charger. He'd driven to Charleston and parked at the Citadel Mall. Alessio would drop him off there for his drive back to Atlanta.

"Who are those guys?" Eddie asked.

"None of your business," Sanborn replied and gave him the baggie with the key in it. "Do you know where Gino Vitale's salvage yard is?"

"Yeah," Jimmy answered. "Out in Goose Creek, right?"

"Right. On Hall Road. Gino's expecting a car to be delivered to him later today. Mr. Coppola wants you to drive that Honda out there and give it to him. He'll get rid of it. You do this, and you forget you did it. Understand?"

"Sure. No problem, Jimmy," the kid said. "Do I get a couple of bucks for this?"

Sanborn put both of his giant hands on Russo's shoulders. "I know you're new around here, Eddie, so here's some advice. If Mr. Coppola asks you to do something, and you ask for money, you're asking for trouble. Capisce?"

"Okay, okay. I got it. Does Gino know what kind of car he's getting?"

"I don't think so, but that doesn't make any difference. Just drive the car out there and make sure Gino gets it."

"How am I gonna get home?"

"Gino will have someone from his shop drive you back to your place. Remember to keep your mouth shut about this."

After returning to the bar, Eddie downed the last of his beer and walked back to the Honda. He thought the shit-brown color sucked, but it looked in good shape besides some dings and scratches. He slid into the driver's seat, removed the key from the baggie, and started the engine. The odometer read 61,375 miles. The interior wasn't that clean, but it seemed to be in decent shape. He went through the glove compartment and was surprised to find the car's title. The title listed the Honda as a 2012 LX Coupe.

He drove out of the bar and headed down Rivers Avenue towards Goose Creek. Eddie knew the car would be chopped for its parts and probably crushed at Gino's shop. *What a fricking waste*, he thought. His car was a 2008 Chevy Malibu with almost 120,000 miles on her. Both rear shocks were gone, and it was on its last leg. Plus, it had been in a few fender benders, and its lower side panels were rusting through. He'd be lucky to get $1,200 for it.

"What the hell," he said out loud and turned into a McDonald's at the intersection of Rivers and Ashley Phosphate. He bought two cheeseburgers and a Coke and pulled into a parking spot. *All right, think this thing through*, he thought.

Eddie figured he might be able to give Gino the Malibu and keep the Honda. He remembered Jimmy said he didn't think Gino knew what kind of car he was getting from Mr. Coppola. Plus, he had a few burner phones and two phony driver's licenses, so there'd be no problem fudging the back of the title and selling the Honda.

Even if Gino was expecting the Honda, Eddie could play dumb and say he got confused. He'd still have time to drive back to his place and get the Honda.

He used his cell phone to search Kelly Blue Book and found out he should get $7,000 for the Honda. If he sold the sucker, he could buy a halfway decent ride and put a couple grand in his pocket. It was too good to pass up. Rather than continuing to Gino's, he drove back to his house and rummaged through his stuff until he found the title for his car. He drove the Malibu out to the salvage yard and delivered it to Gino without any questions.

Eddie Russo created a bogus Facebook page and put the Honda on Facebook Marketplace the following morning. He was surprised when he got a message thirty minutes later from a guy asking about the Honda.

CHAPTER 2

RYAN WOODS WAS a week into a well-deserved two-and-a-half-month summer break from his job as a science teacher at Charleston's West Ashley High School. He'd just finished showering and was getting dressed after a quick late afternoon workout at Planet Fitness when his cell rang. He glanced at the number and saw it was his best friend, Vince Kelly. Ryan was expecting his call. After serving nine years in the Marine Corps, the last five in Special Operations Command, Vince had retired from active duty. Most of his deployments were in Afghanistan and Yemen. As part of the Special OPS team, Vince was called upon to use his unconventional combat skills in counterterrorism and special reconnaissance operations. Much of what he did during his military service was classified and involved cross-border interventions that often required deadly enemy interaction. Like most Marine Raiders, Vince rarely, if ever, spoke about what he'd done during his career in the Marine Corps.

Seeing Vince Kelly on the street, you'd never guess he had just left the military life. His dark brown hair was long but neatly kept, and he had only recently shaved off his full beard. Special ops soldiers resembled anything but military. Their covert missions require them to blend in with the locals, especially in parts of the world where a man's social and political standing are judged by his beard. Vince also looked nothing like the nineteen-year-old kid that showed up at North Charleston's Marine Recruiting Station almost nine years ago. At that time, he was an overweight, muscle-bound, wide-eyed kid with significant self-esteem issues emanating from a father that was gone more than he was home. He'd dropped a good 40 pounds while in the service—his physique totally unrecognizable from the day he enlisted. Like many soldiers who have seen sustained combat, pent-up energy churned below the surface. Even more than his physical metamorphosis was the change in his eyes—eyes that had seen more than their share of inhumanity. Visions of the brutality of war constantly lurked in the corners of his mind. However, for the most part, he'd been able to compartmentalize his military experiences—despite the unsettling nightmares and occasional flashbacks that seemed so real.

"Welcome back, buddy. When did you get in?" Ryan asked.

"I flew in from Pensacola late last night. Katy and I just met with the lawyer, and it's finally done."

"Are you serious? How'd it go?"

Vince chuckled. "It's a no-contest divorce, buddy, so Katy and I just let the lawyer ramble on before signing the papers. There was a discussion about Katy wanting to use her maiden name, Pryor, in the future, but she agreed to keep using our last name on things like her current bank accounts, credit cards, and apartment lease in the short term. Other than those, she wanted to be referred to as Katy Pryor. That got straightened out, and the whole thing took only about twenty-five minutes—all very nice and civil. Katy even gave me a hug and a kiss on the cheek before leaving the lawyer's office for her real estate firm. Oh, and she sends her best. I told her I'd be staying with you until I get settled."

"Are you okay with everything?" Ryan asked. "I mean with how the settlement worked out?"

Vince laughed. "Ryan, we were only married three years— no kids, no mortgage, no vacation home on the beach. We split the money in the joint savings account—which wasn't all that much. She'll get everything in our Mt. Pleasant apartment, and I'll have to pay half the rent until the lease is up. Oh, and she also got the car. That was about it."

"I'm sorry it didn't work out," Ryan said. "I really liked Katy."

"Yeah, I know. Who knows why we didn't make it? Being overseas sure as hell didn't help. We're both fairly independent, and I think we just expected too much of each other. Anyway, we'll stay good friends, and that's a hell of a lot more than most people who split can say." Vince laughed again. "I guess we didn't stay together long enough to hate each other."

Ryan smiled. "Yeah, and the fact that you're both hard-headed didn't help. So, what are you going to do now?"

"Well, I'm out of the apartment, so I need to find a place to live. Plus, I've got to buy a car. And it wouldn't hurt to find a job."

"Like I said, you can crash at my duplex in West Ashley until you find an apartment."

"Thanks, I really appreciate that," Vince said.

"No problem. Where are you now?"

"I'm still at the Halstead Law Firm by the Citadel Mall."

"Stay put. I'll google it and be there in about twenty minutes. I say we pick up a case of beer and head back to my place. We can get you settled and talk about finding you an apartment and some wheels."

"Sounds good," Vince laughed. "I'll pay for the beer; you can provide the electricity."

Ryan Woods and Vince Kelly grew up together in Mt. Pleasant, South Carolina. Their friendship was solidified in the sixth grade when Ryan was walking home from his fourth-grade classes and ran into three middle school assholes. The boys started hassling Ryan and had roughed him up pretty good before Vince showed up. Vince was not only sizable for his age but had grown up in a family that valued toughness. Vince took a hefty beating himself, but he doled out enough damage to the middle schoolers to save Ryan from an even worst drubbing.

Both boys were excellent athletes in high school—Ryan excelling in basketball and baseball while Vince earned his stripes on the football field. In his senior year, Vince was awarded second-team All-State honors as a defensive end on Wando High School's football team. Not to be outdone, Ryan led his

Warriors' baseball team to the conference championship and was named the All-Conference shortstop. Ryan had always been an excellent student and attended Winthrop University in Rock Hill, South Carolina, earning his teaching degree. Vince had a slew of college football scholarship offers but decided to enlist in the Marines right out of high school. His father and grandfather had both served in the Marine Corps, and there was never any doubt Vince would follow in their footsteps.

With Ryan away at school and Vince deployed overseas, the boys didn't see much of each other. They did, however, stay in contact whenever possible. Time had done little to diminish their bond.

Ryan pulled up in front of the lawyer's office, and Vince tossed his large two-strap, camouflaged Marine Duffle Bag in the back seat of Ryan's Silverado and got in. They stopped at the grocery store and picked up the case of beer, chips, and two steaks. Ryan put the beer and food in his back seat when he noticed Vince's bag. "Is that everything you got?"

Shortly after Katy and he were married, Vince rented a storage unit to keep certain items he didn't want Katy to know about. "No. I've got one of those self-storage places out on Ashley River Road." He gestured toward his Duffle Bag. "That'll get me by until I find a place to live."

Ryan gave Vince an extra key to his apartment. "Well, like I said, you can stay at my place as long as you need to. Now, let's see if we can put a dent in that case of beer."

~~~~
~~~~

The following morning, Ryan rolled out of bed at eight o'clock and was surprised to see Vince sitting at the kitchen table wearing a U.S. Marine T-shirt drenched in sweat. He'd sandwiched his regular five-mile run between fifty finger pushups and a hundred leg lifts.

"Jesus, Vince, don't tell me you've been out running already."

"Yep. I try to do about five miles every morning. Old habits are tough to break. Plus, if I remember correctly, we drank a hell of a lot of beer last night, and I wanted to sweat it out."

"You're right about the beer," Ryan said, "but I prefer to deal with my hangovers with aspirin, scrambled eggs, hash browns, and a few cups of black coffee."

Ryan made breakfast while Vince showered and dressed. They ate and spent the next hour looking through Craigslist and Facebook Marketplace for apartments. Vince found a few possibilities they planned on visiting that afternoon.

"Now, let's see if we can find you a car," Ryan said.

Vince was checking Facebook Marketplace when he said, "Ryan, take a look at this one." He was looking at a photo of a 2012 Honda Civic listed for $7,000. "It's only got about 60,000 miles. It's more than I wanted to spend, but it might be worth looking at. What do you think?"

"Definitely," Ryan said. "How much can you spend?"

"Not a whole lot. Katy and I dumped a fair piece of change into getting her real estate company up and running. I've got about $15,000 in the bank, but I figure at least $3,000 will go toward the apartment's rent and security deposit—plus I got to pay half of Katy's rent for the next four months. I'll need a bed and some furniture. I don't know how long it'll take to find a job, and I don't want to strap myself. I was thinking a max of about $6,000 for the car."

"Why don't you just send the guy a message and get more information on the Honda. If it sounds good, we can take a look at it."

Vince responded to the Marketplace ad, and after going back and forth with a few more messages, he got the person's information and agreed to meet him at the Centre Point Apartments in North Charleston that morning at 10:30.

~~~~

Eddie Russo picked the Centre Point Apartments to meet the guy inquiring about the Honda because the girlfriend of one of his buddies lived there. Eddie knew the apartment would be empty because she'd gone to Atlanta with his friend for the weekend. He was waiting next to the Honda in the apartment's parking lot when Ryan and Vince arrived. Eddie knew they would be in a black Silverado and waved at the truck when he saw it pulling in.

"There's he is," Vince said and told Ryan to park the Silverado a few spaces from the Honda. "The car looks okay from here. Let's check it out."

Ryan noticed a small university sticker on the rear windshield of the Honda. He pointed at the car and said, "Look
~~~~

at that sticker. The guy must have gone to the University of South Carolina."

They got out of the truck and saw what looked like a kid standing next to the Civic. Vince introduced himself and Ryan and, after a few questions about the car, asked, "Do you mind if we take it for a spin?"

"Sure," Eddie replied. "The keys are in it. I'll just wait here."

Vince had just turned onto I-526 when Ryan commented that the car hadn't been washed, and while the interior looked okay, it could definitely use a good cleaning. Despite this, it drove smoothly with no obvious mechanical issues. Vince pulled off the freeway into Lowe's parking lot, popped the hood, and quickly inspected the engine. He could find no apparent problems.

They made it back to Centre Point Apartments about ten minutes later. "The car drove okay," Vince said to the kid. "If I can ask, why are you selling it?"

Eddie figured he'd be asked that and had come up with a story. "I just moved here from Columbia, and the job I got includes a car. So, I don't need the Honda anymore."

"I'll be perfectly honest with you," Vince began. "I hadn't planned on spending that much. Would you be willing to work with me on the price?"

"That depends on what you're willing to offer."

"I just got out of the Marines, and all I can handle is $6,000. If that works for you, I can get you a certified check from the bank this morning."

"Hey, man," Eddie responded, "I checked Kelly Blue Book, and it said I should get around seven thousand bucks for it."

"Maybe so, but that's all I can afford."

Eddie let out his breath and didn't immediately respond. He was disappointed with the offer, but what the hell? If he got the $6,000, he could still pocket a grand after getting himself a decent car. "I'll tell you what," he said, "if you give me the $6,000 in cash now, I'll do it."

Vince almost laughed at the kid. "I don't have that kind of money on me. I said I can go to my bank and get you a certified check."

Eddie was using a fake name and knew he couldn't take a check of any kind. "I want cash," he said. "You can get cash from the bank."

Ryan pulled Vince away from Eddie and whispered, "I doubt you'll find anything as good at that price. I'd tell him you want to see the title, and if everything seems on the up and up, I think you should get the cash and buy the car."

Vince returned to where Eddie was standing. "Okay, but I'd like to see the title if you don't mind," Vince said.

"No problem," he said. "It's in my apartment. Wait here, and I'll be right back." Eddie had put the title under the mat in front of the door to his friend's girlfriend's apartment. He waited a few minutes before returning to the parking lot. "Here you go," he said and gave Vince the title.

He looked it over and handed it to Ryan.

After checking it over, Ryan said it looked legit to him.

"All right," Vince said to the kid, "my bank is open until noon today. I'll get the cash and be back in about forty-five minutes. What's your apartment number?"

"Just call me when you're on your way back," Eddie quickly answered. "I'll meet you out here."

Vince glanced at Ryan, and he nodded. "That works," Vince said. "We'll be back in less than an hour."

It took about forty-five minutes to get to his bank and withdraw the cash. On the way back, Ryan told Vince to get a leather portfolio in his truck's back seat. "There's some paper and a pen in there. Write out a quick bill of sale for the Honda. Leave blanks for the VIN number, the addresses, and a place for both your signatures."

"What address should I use for the bill of sale and title?" Vince asked. "Remember Katy's still living at our apartment in Mt. Pleasant, and I won't be there anymore."

"I know, but I'd go ahead and use that address anyway— your driver's license and all your other identification list the Mt. Pleasant address. I'm sure Katy won't care. You can change it after moving into the new apartment and going to the DMV to pay the sales tax and registration fee. You'll need a new driver's license anyway."

Ryan called the number the guy had given Vince and told him they be back in a few minutes. Eddie Russo, who used the name, James Alexander, met them when they returned. The title and a simple bill of sale were filled out and signed. Vince gave Eddie Russo the six-grand, got the key and title to the Honda, and followed Ryan out of the lot and back to the duplex.

~~~~

After dropping off the Honda at Ryan's, the boys spent most of the afternoon checking out several apartment complexes—finally deciding on the last available one-bedroom unit in West Ashley at a place called Grand Oaks. That unit was being renovated and would not be ready for Vince to move into until mid-to-late July. That worked out better for Vince since his first month's rent and the security deposit would not be due immediately.

They got back to the duplex around four o'clock. "Let's give your new wheels a bath," Ryan suggested. "I was surprised the guy didn't even clean it up. I'll get a bucket, some rags, and cleaning supplies."

As soon as the exterior was finished, Vince started on the interior, and Ryan worked on the trunk.

Ryan popped the trunk and found a few clumps of dried mud and a good-sized dark stain in the center of the carpet. "Jesus Christ, what a mess!" He used his hands to remove the larger clumps and sucked up what was left of the dirt with the hand vac. There was no way he would get all the stain out—even after scrubbing it several times with soap and water. He finally gave up and began helping Vince finish with the interior.

Vince was vacuuming the carpet under the front seat when he caught sight of a small piece of paper lodged between the front seat and the center console. It was hardly noticeable, and when he tried to get to it, he realized his hands were too large.
~~~~

"Hey, Ryan, come here a minute." Ryan set aside the cloth and glass cleaner and joined Vince in the car's front seat area. Vince pointed under the front seat. "See that paper? Can you reach it?"

Ryan bent down and slid his hand between the console and the metal frame at the bottom of the front seat. He could barely get to it, but he was finally able to pull it out after a few tries. He'd crumpled it up when Vince asked him what was on it.

Ryan smoothed it out. "It's an address." He passed it to Vince.

The piece of paper was small, and Vince had to look close to read it. "It says, *Cornell Jackson, 2131 Stall Road, #8, Tri-County Apts.*" Vince figured he would pitch it when he finished with the car and stuffed it in his jean pocket.

Vince got out of the car and stretched his back. "Hell, Ryan, she cleans up pretty good, doesn't she?"

"Yeah, it looks like a different car."

The guys were putting away the rags and cleaning supplies when Vince mentioned he would need to call his insurance agent on Monday.

"Right," Ryan agreed, "but there's no rush on the DMV. You've got forty-five days to do it. It's almost six o'clock. I could use a couple beers and something to eat. How about we head inside?"

"I thought you'd never ask," Vince replied with a smile.

CHAPTER 3

NOAH MARTIN'S 280-ACRE farm had been in the family for four generations. It was located about 40 miles from Charleston off Highway 17 South in Colleton County. Noah raised a small herd of beef cattle; however, his main cash crop was feed corn.

Like most days, Noah was up this Sunday morning at 4:30. He planned on doing some wild hog hunting before taking his wife, Elizabeth, to church. For years, these wild hogs—often called feral pigs—had done significant damage to his corn crops, spread disease, and polluted the streams and ponds on his and his neighbors' land. The hogs ate his corn and damaged his fields with their rooting, trampling, and wallowing behaviors. A few of his neighbor farmers' livestock had recently been hit with an outbreak of Bovine tuberculosis caused by these hogs.

He'd been tracking one of these troublemakers for about twenty minutes through a densely wooded portion of his land when he heard the familiar sound of hog grunts and snorts coming from about thirty yards up ahead. Noah swung the Winchester Model 70 .30-06 off his shoulder and moved forward quickly and stealthily as possible. When he reached the top of a slight rise, he saw what must have been a 250-pound adult male hog digging in the ground. After removing his night goggles, Noah took his time lining up the animal in the crosshairs of his night vision scope. He knew he'd only get one shot. He slowly let his breath out, held it, and pulled the trigger. The hog jumped as the bullet entered its right shoulder. It shrieked, stumbled, and took off running.

Noah knew these hogs were one of the toughest animals to kill, but he was surprised the beast hadn't gone down. He scrambled to his feet and began jogging after the animal. But as he passed the spot where the hog was digging, he stopped dead in his tracks.

"Sweet mother of Jesus," he whispered.

A human arm protruded from the dirt at the bottom of the trough the hog had opened. Noah stumbled back and, after a few tries, got his cell phone out of the pocket in his overalls and called the County Sheriff's office.

The call rang three times before the on-duty officer answered, "Colleton County Sheriff's office. Officer Mike Brown speaking."

Noah's hand continued to shake, and his breathing quickened. He tried hard not to drop the phone. "Mike, it's Noah Martin. I got a dead body here."

~~~~
~~~~

The Colleton County Sheriff's office was in Waterboro—about six miles from Noah's farm. The sun was coming up by the time a deputy made it out to the Martin farmhouse. Sheriff Seth Johansson showed up twenty minutes later. Noah and Elizabeth were on the porch when Sheriff Johansson arrived. Noah told his wife to stay put and met the sheriff when he got out of his cruiser.

Johansson took off his hat and nodded to Elizabeth Martin before acknowledging her husband. "Morning, Noah. Officer Brown tells me you found more than you bargained for this morning. Tell me what we've got here."

Noah began explaining what had happened when two more county police cars arrived at the farmhouse. Sheriff Johansson instructed his officers to contact EMS and Doc Wilson, the county coroner. After Noah gave Johansson a quick recap of what had happened earlier that morning, the two rode Noah's ATV as far as they could and walked the rest of the way to where he'd shot the hog. There was no mistaking when they got to where the body was found—the smell was overpowering.

A hanky covered Noah's nose and mouth as he approached the hole. The sheriff stopped him. "Hold it right there, Noah." He pointed to the dug-up area. "This here's a crime scene."

"Sorry. I swear I hit that hog dead-center, and I almost tripped over this when I started after it. I just about crapped my pants when I saw that arm sticking up. It was almost like it was pointing at me. It was like one of those horror movies. Still got the willies."

Johansson used his cell to take several pictures from various angles before putting on elastic gloves and approaching the body. He bent down to inspect the arm. It was bloated. The sheriff gently tied to move the arm, but the signs of rigor mortis were still present.

"How long do you think it's been here?" Noah asked.

"Hard to tell. It's been buried, so I figure it could have been up to a few days. The coroner will give me a better idea once the body is dug up and back to the county lab. Let's get back to your place. I want my officers out here to tape off the area and make sure it stays secure until the coroner and forensics okay its removal."

CHAPTER 4

IT DIDN'T TAKE long until local TV stations and newspapers broadcasted the gruesome find in Colleton County. The following Monday evening, Charleston's Live5 News Channel was in Walterboro interviewing Sheriff Johansson for their six o'clock news.

The television was on in the background while Vince and Ryan ate sandwiches and talked about possible places Vince might find a job. Ryan had just left to get two more beers when Vince heard the words, *Cornell Jackson.* That name sounded vaguely familiar. He glanced up at the TV and listened to a reporter say something about a body being found buried on a farm. Then it hit him.

Son-of-a-bitch! Vince thought and called out, "Ryan! Get back here."

"I'm getting some more beer, dude. I'll be there in a minute."

Jesus Christ, Vince thought, *was that the name on that piece of paper I found in the Honda?*

Ryan walked back into the living room and handed Vince a beer. "What'd you want?"

"Hang on a second," he said. "I'll be right back," Vince remembered he'd stuffed that note in the jeans he wore when they were cleaning the Honda. He put down the beer and quickly left for his bedroom. He found the jeans. The note was still there. "Damn," he whispered when he saw the name *Cornell Jackson* written on the paper.

"So, what is it?" Ryan asked when Vince returned to the living room.

"Remember that note we found in the Honda?" Vince asked.

"Sure, what about it?"

Vince held up the piece of paper. "Cornell Jackson."

"Yeah, so what," Ryan said, a bit confused.

Vince explained he was positive he'd just heard Cornell Jackson's name on a TV news report. It was something about a buried body found on a farm, and the body was identified as someone named Cornell Jackson.

"Wait a second," Ryan said. "So, you're saying someone with the same name on that note was found dead and buried on some farm?"

"That's exactly what I'm saying!"

Vince flipped the channel until he found the NBC affiliate. A few minutes later, the news anchor began reporting about a body found on a farm in Colleton County. The victim's body was identified as Cornell Jackson.

Ryan was stunned. "What the hell?"

"What the hell is right!" Vince said. "What does a guy who was murdered and buried have to do with that note in the Honda?"

"Exactly. This is messed up! I still don't get it."

"There's got to be a connection," Vince said. "That kid I bought the car from has to be involved. Hell, it was his car."

"We need to call the police," Ryan said.

"You're right, but that means I'll probably lose the Honda and the six-grand I paid for it. I need to have a little talk with that guy before we do anything with the cops."

"So, what do we do?" Ryan asked.

"What do you think?" Vince was out of his chair and heading for the door. "I'm going to get my money back, leave the damn car with the kid, and call the cops. Are you coming?"

"Of course," Ryan said and grabbed his keys. "I'll follow you in the truck."

Vince was about to get into the Honda when Ryan asked him if he had the car's title and his copy of the bill of sale.

"Yeah, they're both still in the glove compartment."

"What address did the kid put on the bill of sale?" Ryan asked.

"Hang on," Vince opened the glove compartment and retrieved the bill of sale and the title.

"Did he put an apartment number on it?" Ryan asked.

"Damn it, he didn't!"

"But I remember the building he went into to get the title."

"All right, I'll meet you there," Ryan said. "We can at least check the apartments in that building."

It was a short ten-minute drive to the Centre Point Apartments. Vince pulled in first and was followed by Ryan. They parked in front of the building where they'd met the kid. When he exited the Honda, Vince had both the title and bill of sale in hand. He met Ryan, and the two walked to the building's entrance.

"How do you want to handle this?" Ryan asked.

The numbers on the front of the building listed twelve individual apartments: four on each of the three floors.

"It's Monday evening," Vince observed. "You've got to figure most of the tenants are probably home. Let's just knock on the doors and see if the guy answers. If someone else lives there, we just ask them if they know which apartment James Alexander lives in."

Vince knocked on the first door to his right. He waited a few seconds and knocked again—louder this time.

There was the sound of a lock being disengaged, and the door, held back by a security chain, opened a few inches. A young woman appeared.

"Yes?" she said, her face showing a hint of uneasiness.

"I'm sorry to bother you," Vince said. "We're looking for a James Alexander."

"Sorry, don't know him," the woman now sounded perturbed and quickly shut her door.

Vince moved on to the apartment to his left. It was answered by an elderly gentleman who also knew nothing of James Alexander. The next apartment went unanswered, and they moved through the remaining apartments without any indication that a James Alexander lived in the building.

"I can't say I'm surprised the kid didn't live here," Ryan said. "I'm sorry, buddy. I should have known better. I think we got hustled."

"It's my fault," Vince replied. "Six-grand for a car like that? I should have known better. I bet the sucker was stolen." He half-laughed. "I'm driving around in stolen property. I guess that makes me a criminal. So, what do we do now?"

"Let's go back to my place," Ryan suggested. "There are sites we can use to search the license plate and VIN number that'll tell us who actually owns the car."

Back at the duplex, Ryan pulled up a site on his computer that identified an auto's owner based on the DMV-issued license plate. The result wasn't surprising. The license number was attached to a Mr. Charles Gantry of Summerville.

"I'll bet the license plate was stolen," Vince offered. "Check the VIN number."

Ryan punched in the seventeen letters and numbers of the VIN that appeared on the title. The result was also no surprise. The owner of the car was Susan Rollins of Columbia, South Carolina. It matched the name and address that appeared on the front of the title.

Vince was looking over Ryan's shoulders at the computer screen. "Well, ain't that a son-of-a-bitch? Looks like both the car and the license were stolen."

"I'm afraid you're right, and I think we're screwed. You can probably say goodbye to your six-grand. Hell, Vince, you've got a stolen car with stolen license plates that might have been used in the murder."

"All right," Ryan agreed, "we can do that, but I've got another idea. Remember Russ Riggs?"

"You mean the Russ Riggs we went to high school with?"

"Exactly," Ryan said. "He's been working for the Post & Courier newspaper since he graduated from the College of Charleston. He's bound to know more about this Cornell Jackson character and maybe even why he was murdered."

"Do you have his number?" Vince asked.

"Yeah. A group of us meet every month or two at the Kickin' Chicken to drink beer and talk about the glory days. I can give him a call."

"Wait a minute," Vince said. "What are you going to say? 'Hey, Russ, Vince Kelly just bought a stolen car that had a note in it with the name of that guy that was murdered and buried out on a farm.'"

"Well, that's pretty much what you did," Ryan said with a half-smile. "Think about it. You're eventually going to have to turn the car into the police, right?"

"Yeah, I suppose so."

"Face it, Vince, this is already a big news story. Hell, it was on the evening news. Russ is a reporter. You know he'd love to get in on this thing. I'll just call him and say you're back in town and would like to get together."

"All right," Vince agreed, "but don't say anything about the car or the note."

"I won't."

Ryan made the call. Russ was surprised to hear that Vince was back in town and agreed to meet the following day for lunch at the Warehouse Restaurant downtown at the corner of Spring and St. Philip.

Ryan disconnected the call and eyed at his watch. "It's still early. If you're hell-bent on checking, we can swing by the address on the note and see what the neighborhood looks like."

"Let's do it," Vince said. "Couldn't hurt. Plus, it might give us an idea of what kind of guy this Cornell Jackson is … or was, I guess."

"What kind of guy?" Ryan asked. "He was the kind of guy that gets murdered. That's the kind of guy he was."

"You know what I mean," Vince answered.

"Why don't you leave the Honda here?" Ryan offered. "It's only a ten-minute drive, and we can go in my truck."

Vince locked the Honda, and Ryan asked what the address was on the note.

Vince checked and gave him the Stall Road address. Ryan plugged it into Google Maps and headed east on I-26, getting off at Ashley Phosphate Road. They were on Stall Road a few minutes later, driving past the Tri-County Apartments.

"Not the greatest neighborhood in Charleston," Ryan observed. "More like a Third World country."

"Yeah," Vince answered, "but God knows I've seen worse. Some places in the Middle East are like another planet." By now, the sun had set, leaving only the crimson remnants of the day. "Let's get out of here. This is all I need to see."

CHAPTER 5

RYAN AND VINCE showed up at the Warehouse Restaurant at noon the next day. Russ Riggs was already seated, and after the mandatory handshakes and man-hugs were out of the way, they took their seats. After ordering a round of iced tea, Russ looked surprised when he took in Vince's chiseled 6'2", 220-pound frame. Russ hadn't seen Vince since high school and remembered him as a muscle-bound, 260-pound guy carrying a good portion of that poundage around his mid-section.

"Damn, Kelly, look at you!"

Vince merely smiled and replied, "Nine years of your tax dollars at work. It's good to see you, Russ. Ryan tells me you're a regular Woodward and Bernstein these days."

"I don't know about that, but I'm having fun. Ryan told me you're home for good. What are your plans?"

"Find a place to stay, get a job, and I'll take it from there."

Lunch was ordered, and the boys reminisced about the girls they'd dated and the crazy things they'd done during their high school years.

Vince started to laugh. "Hey, Ryan. Remember that Saturday I told my mom I was sleeping at your house, and you told yours you were spending the night at mine."

"Hell, how could I forget," Ryan answered with a laugh of his own.

Vince picked up the story. "So, Russ, Grace Washburn and Sue Miller told their parents the same thing we told ours. The plan was to meet up at around midnight, drink some beer, and you can imagine the rest. We both got back to our houses around nine Sunday morning. I remember my mom asked me how our little sleepover went. I told her it was okay and that we'd watched TV and played cards."

Ryan chimes in, "Our moms met at the grocery store a few days later. My mom thanked Vince's mom for having me spend the night at her house. It didn't take long for them to figure out what we tried to get away with."

"We both got grounded for a week," Vince added.

The waiter had just cleared away their plates and glasses, and there was a lull in the conversation. Ryan glanced at Vince and said, "Vince and I have something to tell you, but we'd like it to stay between us until we figure out a few things."

Russ grinned and said, "That's a hell of a thing to say to a newspaper reporter, but my lips are sealed. Off the record. Let's hear it."

Ryan explained what had happened with the purchase of the Honda and the problematic situation in which Vince found himself. He then mentioned the news report of the man found murdered in Colleton County.

"Yeah, that's going to be a big story," Russ said. "The paper is gearing up to run with it." Russ tilted his head—waiting for a connection between the Honda and the murdered man. "I get the feeling there's more to your story about Vince's car."

Ryan again glanced at Vince, and Vince nodded. "Okay," Ryan started, "here's where we need your help." He went on to tell Russ how they'd found the note in the Honda with Jackson's name and address on it.

Russ said nothing for a moment, trying to get his head around what he'd just heard. "Jesus."

"Yeah," Vince said. "We figure this Jackson guy must have been into some pretty serious stuff to get murdered. Do you know anything about him or what he was involved in?"

Russ was still floored with everything he'd just heard. "I'm on the political side of the newsroom, but I have a general understanding of Charleston's crime scene—not the particulars, though. Like everything, it's changing all the time. I've never heard of Cornell Jackson, but if you're willing to work only with the Post & Courier on this, I can hook you up with Art Garnett. He heads up our crime desk."

"We're eventually going to have to tell the police," Ryan said.

"Of course," Russ agreed. "I'm only talking about news outlets. What you two just fell into adds a whole new twist to the murder story."

"Okay," Vince said, "but we need to keep our names out of it?"

"That would be up to Art, but he's a hell of a reporter and protects his sources. If that works for you, I'll give him a call right now."

Ryan glanced at Vince. "Do it," Vince said.

Russ got ahold of Garnett and told him he knew individuals with new information about the Colleton County murder. He listened for a moment, disconnected the call, and said, "Art said he's already had over a dozen crank calls about the murder, but I vouched for you guys. You're in. He told me to bring you to his office now, and he'll listen to what you have to say."

The restaurant was only a few blocks from the Post & Courier building, and the three of them arrived there ten minutes later. Russ introduced Ryan and Vince and left. Garnett ushered them into his office.

Garnett was the opposite of what the boys expected of someone intimately involved in Charleston's various criminals and their alliances. They expected an older, tough-looking guy with sleeves rolled up and his tie loosened. But Garnett's features betrayed their expectations. He was a short man seeming to be in his early thirties, his hair longish, wearing an obviously tailored suit.

Garnett took a seat behind his desk and asked, "So gentlemen, what do you have for me?"

Over the next ten minutes, Ryan and Vince noted the series of events that led them to believe that the Honda may have been used in the murder of Cornell Jackson.

"Both the license plate and the car were stolen," Vince said. "The guy's name I bought the car from was James Alexander. That was not his real name, and he didn't live in the apartments he said he did."

Vince was about to say something else when Ryan leaned forward and asked if Garnett knew Cornell Jackson or who might have killed him.

"That seems to be the question, doesn't it?" Garnett responded. "I've heard of Jackson, but before I get into that, let me give you a brief overview of the different criminal groups active in our town. Like any medium to large city, we've got our street gangs, a chapter of the Hell's Angels, and even a smattering of MS-13, but the major organized players here in Charleston continue to be the Sinaloa Cartel, the Russians, and the Mafia.

"These three main groups are in a state of flux. While they continue to be ruthless, the Russians have evolved primarily into areas of white-collar crimes—like corporate fraud, embezzlement, Ponzi schemes, and extortion. A few years ago, the Feds came down hard on the Sinaloa Cartel and the local Mafia. Both have been substantially weakened. For years, most of the Charleston area's criminal activity was controlled by the Santoro family—an offshoot of the Chicago Mafia. However, a notorious hitman known as the Sandman was captured, and his testimony resulted in multiple RICO indictments and convictions of mafia bosses in Charleston and Chicago. Several mid-level bosses in Charleston survived the indictments. Despite this, it didn't take long before gangs began infiltrating many neighborhoods previously controlled by the Santoro family.

"Both the Sinaloa Cartel and the local mafia have begun to rebuild their organizations. Two years ago, the Chicago Outfit sent one of their lieutenants by the name of Frank Romano to Charleston and a man named Alessio Messina to reorganize their operations here. Romano was a bodyguard and enforcer for the Chicago underboss, Salvatore Cataudella. In his younger years, Romano was given the nickname 'Fingers' due to his reputation of breaking the middle finger of individuals who refused or could not pay their debt to the Outfit.

"As you can imagine, the crime task force and the FBI have been monitoring Romano's activities since he showed up in Charleston. And so have I. He operates out of a small import business in Westview Industrial Park in North Charleston called AC Global Imports. I've learned that Romano is a creature of habit. He arrives at his business almost every morning at eleven. Messina joins him around two in the afternoon. The few employees working at the company leave like clockwork at five Monday through Friday. Also, he flies to Chicago once a month to meet with Cataudella. While he's up there, he sees his daughter, Teresa, who is a junior at Northwestern."

Vince made a mental note of Romano's consistent arrivals and departures from his business. He would also need to recon the building Romano operated out of.

"Are you saying this Frank Romano is responsible for Cornell Jackson's murder?" Ryan asked.

"I didn't say that, now did I?" Garnett quickly responded. He swiveled around in his chair and pointed to a large map of the greater Charleston metropolitan area. The map outlined and identified individual neighborhoods. Colored pins showed what gang or criminal organization controlled a particular area.

"Here's what I do know. Several small local crime operations report to Romano. One of these is run by Michael Coppola. Coppola controls the prostitution, loansharking, and drug business in the Oak Grove, Belvedere, and Highland Park areas of North Charleston. He operates out of a bar called Callaghan's on Dorchester Road. Word is that a small-time hustler named Cornell Jackson has a group of teenagers who have been selling drugs in the Belvedere and Oak Grove neighborhoods."

"If Romano didn't do it, did this Coppola fellow have Jackson killed?" Ryan asked.

"All I'm saying is to use your imagination, gentlemen," Garnett replied. "In some way, that note you found connects Cornell Jackson to the man who sold the car to you. But it doesn't prove Frank Romano, Michael Coppola, or anyone else actually murdered or ordered the murder of Jackson."

"What do we do now?" Vince asked—his voice displaying frustration. "I just paid $6,000 for a stolen car that might have been used in a murder."

Garnett thought a moment. "All right, don't talk to anyone about this. Give me a day to check my sources. I'll let you know what I come up with, but whatever happens, you should definitely go to the police with what you have after we talk tomorrow."

Garnett took down Ryan and Vince's contact information and gave both of them one of his business cards.

"Sit tight on this for the next twenty-four hours," Garnett said. "Hopefully, I'll have something for you tomorrow."

CHAPTER 6

MICHAEL COPPOLA WAS in his office at Callaghan's later that evening watching CNN and nursing a glass of wine when Jimmy Sanborn opened the door. "Boss, you got company."

Coppola switched off the TV, set his wine aside, and told Sanborn to send them in. Sanborn opened the door, and Frank Romano entered, followed by Alessio Messina and another one of Romano's bodyguards by the name of Sammy Amato. Messina was Frank Romano's second in command and a unique combination of brains and brawn. Sammy Amato possessed Alessio's brawn but was seriously lacking in the brain's part of the equation. The two men took positions on either side of the door like two dangerous bookends—their faces absent of even a hint of emotion.

"I'll be outside, boss," Sanborn said and closed the door behind him.

The Colleton County murder had been all over the news, and Coppola knew this was the reason for Romano's visit. He immediately stood and walked around his desk, extending his hand.

Romano ignored the attempted handshake. "Sit down," he ordered, his voice radiating a sense of power like one of those Fortune 500 CEOs. Coppola retreated to his seat. Romano remained standing. "We have a situation here, Michael."

"I understand. The guy that took out Jackson fucked up."

"He did," Romano answered, "but if I remember correctly, you hired him. It's not going to take a genius to figure out Cornell Jackson was playing in your backyard. The cops will connect him to you, and that means it becomes a problem for me. I don't need problems, Michael."

"I know, Frank. I know. But you okayed the job." He immediately knew he'd made a mistake. The two men who had been leaning against the wall straightened up. Romano's face hardened, and his eyes bored into Coppola, who recovered enough to say, "I didn't mean you okayed it, Frank. I just meant …"

"Enough, Michael!" Romano snapped. "Who else knows you hired him?"

Coppola nodded toward Alessio and Sammy. "Only your guys and Jimmy Sanborn," Coppola paused and continued, "There's also a kid who drove the car used in the job out to Gino's place. But the kid doesn't know anything."

"What's his name?" Romano asked.

"Russo," Coppola answered, "Eddie Russo."

"Did Gino get rid of the car?"

"The kid dropped it off Friday. Gino was going to chop it and crush it."

"That's not good enough, Michael." Romano pointed to the phone on Coppola's desk. "Call Gino."

The call was made. Gino answered, and Coppola began questioning him about the status of the Honda Civic the kid was to drop off Friday.

"Hold on, Michael," Gino said. "What's this about a Honda. Your kid dropped off a piece of shit Chevy Malibu."

Coppola was confused. He stuttered a bit before saying, "No, Gino. The kid was supposed to give you a Honda Civic?"

"I just told you your guy dropped off a Chevy. I don't know anything about any Honda. Nick is going to start chopping the Chevy now. You still want it cut up and crushed?"

"No, hold off on that. I'll call you back and let you know."

Coppola hung up—still confused but knowing he'd have to come up with something to tell Romano. There was an uneasy silence before he eventually said, "Gino's thinks the kid dropped off a Chevy Malibu. He's a little confused, Frank. I'll figure out what happened."

Romano said nothing. Coppola could feel the weight of his stare like white-hot embers.

"Cut the bullshit, Michael."

"Okay," Coppola said—aware of the bead of perspiration snaking down the side of his forehead. "I don't know, Frank. I gave the keys to Jimmy, and he told the kid to drive the car out to Gino's. That's all I know."

"Sounds like that never happened." Romano turned around and told Alessio to get Sanborn. Jimmy entered the office, and Romano explained what was going on. "What kind of car does Eddie Russo drive?"

"An old Chevy," Sanborn answered.

There was a tense moment of silence as the entire room connected the dots.

"Do you want Jimmy to bring him in?" asked Coppola.

Romano shot him a repugnant look and said, "No, Michael. You've screwed this up enough. I'll have my boys handle it." He turned his attention to Sanborn and asked where Russo lived.

"He lives with his aunt on Kenwood Drive in the Midland Park area of North Charleston," Sanborn said.

Romano told Alessio to drop him off at his import business located in the Westview Industrial Park. One of Mr. Romano's associates managed the company, but more importantly, it was nothing more than a front for his criminal operations. He told Jimmy Sanborn to go with Alessio and Sammy to pick up the Honda from the kid and get it out to Gino's place. "I want that Honda and that Malibu crushed tonight."

As everyone was leaving the office, Frank Romano pulled Alessio aside. "The kid worries me. Keep your eye on him. Call me when you've gotten rid of the cars."

CHAPTER 7

THE PIZZA BOX was empty, and Ryan and Vince were watching a rerun of Friends when Ryan asked, "As soon as I found out you were coming home, I talked with Katy, and she told me you didn't want to stay with your dad. Tell me if I'm out of line, but what really happened between you two? I know he wasn't around much when we were growing up. But Katy said you haven't talked to him in years."

Ryan's question caught Vince off guard, and it took him a moment to respond. "I don't know—it's hard to say. You know Dad was in the Marines most of his life. He first saw action in the early 90s during Desert Shield and Desert Storm. He has a tattoo of a scorpion and the words Desert Storm on his right forearm. He spent most of his career in Afghanistan and the Middle East. He retired as a First Sergeant when we were in high school. I don't think he ever adjusted to life outside the Corps. He tried a few jobs when he got out, but none of them lasted all that long. My mom divorced him, and he moved into an apartment in North Charleston. I lived with Mom, so I didn't see him all that much, but she told me he'd gotten involved with some shady characters."

"Shady characters?" Ryan asked—raising his eyebrows.

"I don't think she really knew who. Mom never trusted Dad after the divorce."

"What about when you joined the Marines?" Ryan asked. "I mean, did you stay in touch with him?"

"I saw him on and off for the next three years until I was accepted into the Special Operations Command. My MARSOC deployments lasted between six and nine months, so I rarely saw him—the last time was right before Katy and I got married."

"That's right," Ryan said, "I almost forgot. Your dad never showed up for your wedding. Must have been tough on both you and Katy."

"Yeah. You could say that. Anyway, I never heard from him again, and I was too pissed and proud to try. He still lives in the same apartment, but like I said, I haven't had any contact since the wedding."

"Do you know what he's doing?" Ryan asked.

"No," Vince said. "I ask my mom about that whenever we talk, but she doesn't know or care. It is what it is. Anyway, enough of that. What's your best guess about tomorrow? Do you think Garnett will come up with anything?"

"Who knows? But it sure seemed like he knew what he was talking about."

"Yeah, he did," Vince said, "but I figure I'll lose the Honda either way, and I'm out the six-grand. Hell of a way to start my life as a civilian."

Alessio pulled his black Dodge Charger off Midland Park Boulevard onto Kenwood, stopping in front of Eddie Russo's house. He told Sanborn to get the kid and the keys to the Honda.

Sanborn knocked on the front door, and Russo opened it. He was surprised to have Jimmy show up at his house.

"Hey, Jimmy. What's up?"

Sanborn pushed past him. "Where's your aunt?"

"She's at her sister's place. What's up?" he repeated.

"Where's the Honda?"

All Russo could manage was a weak, "What do you mean?"

"Jesus, Eddie, how could you be so stupid? We know about the Malibu. Did you really think no one would notice? Michael is pissed, so don't make it worse than it already is."

Russo slumped into one of the living room chairs but said nothing.

Sanborn took the chair across from him. "Jesus, Eddie, what were you thinking? Talk to me."

The color drained from Russo's face, and he finally answered, "I don't know, Jimmy. You said Gino didn't know what kind of car he was getting. I just figured … I don't know … what's Michael going to do?"

"I don't know," Sanborn quickly answered. "All I know is that now Frank Romano's involved, and he wants the car back. Where is it?"

"I don't have it."

"You don't have it! What the hell does that mean?" Sanborn said—clearly surprised with the answer.

"I sold it, Jimmy."

Now it was Sanborn that was at a loss for words. Finally, he recovered and asked, "Who? Who did you sell it to?"

"Just some guy," Russo mumbled.

Christ, Sanborn thought, *the kid is naïve as a ten-year-old.*

"A name, Eddie. I need a name!"

Russo remembered the bill of sale. "Wait here. I got the guy's name and address." Russo left for his bedroom and returned a moment later. He handed his copy of the bill of sale to Sanborn.

Sanborn read off the buyer's name and address from the bill of sale. "Vincent Kelly, 1900 North Highway 17, # 113, Mt. Pleasant." He saw the sale price. "Six thousand bucks? You got six-grand for the Honda?"

"Yeah," Russo answered.

"Where's the money?"

"In my room, but I already spent five hundred of it."

"Go get it," Sanborn ordered. "The money goes to Mr. Coppola, plus the five hundred you spent."

Russo retrieved the money from his room and handed the envelope to Sanborn. "It's all there, except the five hundred."

"All right," Sanborn said, "come with me. We need to find that Honda."

Russo grabbed his windbreaker and followed Sanborn out of the house. When he got close to the Charger, he saw two men sitting in the car. "Who are those guys?"

"That's Alessio and Sammy. They work for Frank Romano. Now get in the damn car."

Sanborn got in the front, and Russo stepped into the back seat next to Sammy. The kid said, "Hi, I'm Eddie." Sammy ignored him.

"Where's the Honda?" Alessio asked—his voice soft-spoken, betraying his size and countenance. But it still had a chilling effect.

"That's the problem," Sanborn said. "Eddie just told me he sold it. But I got the name and address of the guy who bought it."

Alessio turned around and gave Russo a withering stare. "You stupid son-of-a-bitch."

"I'm sorry," Russo said. "But we know where it is, and it'll be easy to find."

"You got another set of keys to the car?" Alessio asked.

"No, there was only the one Jimmy gave me."

"Give me the address," Alessio said, his voice fuming.

Twenty-five minutes later, they arrived at the Thickett Apartments in Mt. Pleasant. Realizing the apartments probably had security cameras, Alessio parked the Charger across the street in the Towne Centre Shopping Mall.

He told Sammy to stay in the car with Jimmy Sanborn and turned around to face Russo, "I remember the car, but I wasn't paying attention. Tell me about this Honda."

"It's a two-door," Russo answered. "Kind of dark brownish. An older Civic. It's got a small University of South Carolina sticker on the back windshield."

"All right, kid, you come with me, but don't look around. Just keep your head down and your eyes focused on the pavement in front of you." Russo followed Alessio into the complex as he was told, and as they approached apartment #113, the muffled sound of a TV could be heard from inside.

"You know what this guy looks like, right?" Alessio asked.

"Yeah."

"All right, Just let me know if it's him, and I'll handle it."

Russo was about to knock on the apartment door when his cell phone rang. He quickly pulled it from his pants pocket and silenced it. Alessio gave him a toxic stare, and Russo promptly put the phone in the pocket of his windbreaker. Alessio reached in front of Russo and knocked.

Katy was in her pajamas watching TV and doing her nails when she heard the knock on her door.

Alessio and Russo heard locks being released, and the door opened slightly, held by the safety chain. A woman peered out but said nothing.

Expecting Vince Kelly, Russo was surprised to see a woman. He quickly backed away, turned to face Alessio, and whispered, "It ain't him. It's a girl."

Alessio stepped forward and said, "Excuse me. Is Vince Kelly here?"

"He doesn't live here anymore," Katy said and started to shut the door.

For some reason, Russo panicked and slammed his shoulder into the door, tearing the chain from the frame. The door flew open, smashing the side of Katy's face. She was thrown backward—her head colliding with the side of a heavy coffee table. Russo fell forward, tripped, and tumbled onto the living room floor.

"God damn it!" Alessio seethed. "Why the hell did you do that?" He bent down to check the woman. She seemed unconscious—her breathing shallow. There was a gash on the side of her head. Russo had just scrambled to his feet when Alessio ordered, "Watch her and don't touch anything!" He pulled out his Glock 19, stepped around Katy, and began checking the balance of the apartment.

While Alessio was in the bedrooms and bathrooms, Russo eyed Katy's purse on the kitchen counter. He opened it, found two $50s and several $20s, and grabbed the bills. The kid noticed an old necklace on the counter next to the purse. Without thinking, he snatched it and stuffed it in his pocket.

Once Alessio was satisfied no one else was in the place, he returned to the living room. Katy's face was bathed in blood, and a pool of crimson began to form on the carpet at the back of her head.

"I'm sorry," Russo pleaded, "I didn't mean to do that."

"Shut up! Let's get out of here but don't run. Remember, keep your head down and just walk normally." Alessio left the apartment with Russo following in his wake.

As soon as they made it back to the Charger, Russo got in the rear and Alessio behind the steering wheel.

"Did you get the car?" Sanborn asked.

"No! Your boy fucked up," Alessio shot back and explained what occurred at the apartment.

He smacked the car into gear and slammed his foot on the accelerator. Twenty minutes later, he pulled up in front of Callaghan's.

"What's going to happen now?" Russo asked.

"I don't know," Alessio answered. "Both of you, get out!"

When Sanborn and Russo left the Charger, Sammy got out of the back seat and joined his partner in the front. "We need to tell Frank."

"No shit," Alessio replied.

"Did the girl see the kid's face?" Sammy asked.

"Yeah, she probably did."

"How about you?"

Alessio realized he'd screwed up and was pretty sure the girl had seen his face. "I don't know. Maybe."

Alessio put the Charger in gear, but there was a knock on the passenger's side window before he could leave. It was Russo with Sanborn standing behind him.

Sammy lowered the window, and the kid said, "Sorry, guys. I think I left my phone in the back seat."

Alessio slammed the gear shift back into park. "Well, don't just stand there; get it."

Russo opened the rear door, and he and Sanborn began searching. It wasn't on the seat. Russo checked between the seats and the rear doors. No luck. It wasn't on the floor or under the front or back seat. "I can't find it."

"Did you check your pants and jacket?" Sammy asked, his patience running thin.

"Yeah. I remember putting it in my jacket pocket right before we went inside that apartment."

Both Sammy and Alessio got out and began searching the car. Nothing!

Finally, Alessio said, "Damn! It must be back at that girl's place. It probably fell out of your jacket when you broke that door down." He slammed his fist down on the car's roof and said, "Sammy, get in."

"Wait," Russo said. "It's not my regular phone, man. It's just a burner. Ain't got nothing on it."

"Nothing on it?" Alessio said sarcastically. "Your fucking fingerprints are on it. Sanborn, you can take off." He pointed at Russo. "But I don't want you going anywhere. Stay the hell at the bar until we get back!"

Alessio turned the Charger around and headed back to Mt. Pleasant.

He again parked in the mall parking lot. "Sammy, let's go."

CHAPTER 8

KATY HAD LAIN unconscious for a time until her eyes fluttered. She felt confused, and then came the pain—a deep, piercing pain radiating from the side and back of her head. Without thinking, she reached up and touched the side of her face. It felt wet. She tried to sit up, but the pain and dizziness threw her back down. She opened an eye and saw her cell phone under the sofa about six feet away. Dragging herself, she reached the phone and pressed its home button.

"Call Vince," she managed.

"Calling Vince," came the familiar sound of Siri.

Ryan had left to pick up some coffee and milk at the grocery store, and Vince was in the kitchen when he heard his phone ring. He jogged to his bedroom and answered it.

"Hello."

"Help." The voice was slurred and barely audible.

"Katy, is that you?"

"Help," she repeated—almost a whisper.

"What happened?" Vince asked.

"Don't know."

"Katy!" Vince knew something was wrong. "Where are you?"

"Home."

"Are you hurt?"

"I think so. I'm sorry." Again, her voice was like a whisper in the wind.

"Stay on the phone, Katy. I'm coming over there. Can you hear me?"

No answer.

"Katy! Can you hear me?"

No answer.

Still holding his cell, Vince ran out of the bedroom—scooping up the keys to the Honda on the way out of the apartment. He was in the car and about to back up when Ryan pulled in beside him.

"Where are you going?" Ryan asked.

"Something's happened to Katy! I gotta go!"

"What?" Ryan stammered. "Katy?"

"I need to go!"

"Hang on, I'll come with you," Ryan shouted, exited the Silverado, and jumped in the Honda.

They arrived at the apartment complex twenty minutes later. When they got to Katy's apartment, Ryan tried the door, and it swung open, exposing the broken chain and door jam. Vince entered, followed by Ryan. The TV had been turned off, and Katy was now sitting on the living room couch, holding a blood-soaked towel to the side of her head. A weak "Vince" was all she could muster.

"Jesus!" Vince said when he saw her face.

"I called you, didn't I?" Katy asked, her eyes dilated and her voice still wavering.

"What happened to you?"

Katy paused for a second or two, then pulled herself back. "There was a man. He knocked me down."

"When? When did this happen?"

"I was going to bed and heard a knock on the door. When I opened it something hit me. That's all I remember."

Vince carefully removed the blood-soaked towel and inspected the cuts on the side and back of her head. "We need to get you to a doctor."

"I'm not dressed," Katy said.

He started to help her up when Ryan called out to him, "Vince, take a look at this." Ryan was holding up Katy's purse and had her wallet open. Her credit cards were still there, but there was no cash.

Vince nodded, understanding that whatever happened might or might not have been a robbery. He knew Katy always carried at least $200 in cash if she had to entertain one of her real estate clients.

"There's no way Katy's coming back here tonight," Vince said. "She's going to have to stay with us."

"Absolutely," Ryan quickly agreed.

"Thanks. I'm going to help Katy get dressed and pack some of her clothes and personal things." Vince emerged from the bedroom with Katy and a small suitcase a few minutes later. "Ryan, grab her purse. There's a Doctor's Care right down Highway 17. We'll take her there."

~~~~

Alessio and Sammy exited the Charger, crossed Highway 17, and entered the Thickett Apartments. They were approaching Katy's apartment when Alessio noticed a brown car in front of the girl's apartment. He grabbed Sammy. "Hold on!"

"What?" Sammy said.

"The Honda! That's the Honda parked outside the girl's apartment. I remember the kid told me it was brown and had a college sticker on the back window."

"What do we do now?" Sammy said.

"The Honda wasn't there before," Alessio said. "And the girl said this Kelly guy didn't live there anymore. The car's here, and I bet he's inside with her." He thought for a moment. "We wait."

"Why don't we just go in, get the keys, and take the car?" Sammy offered.

"No. First, we don't know how many people are in there, and they may have called the cops. Plus, if we go in, they'll be able to identify us. Whoever is in there has to eventually come out. I say we wait and follow them." Alessio checked his watch. "It's already 10:30. This Vince Kelly guy eventually has to go home. When he does, we follow him and then decide what to do."
~~~~

"Should we call Mr. Romano?" Sammy asked.

"Do you want to tell him how fucked up this situation is?" Alessio answered with a frown. "I say we fix it and then call him. We wait."

~~~~

When they arrived at the emergency facility, Vince helped Katy fill out the necessary insurance and medical forms. No one else was in the waiting room, and as soon as the forms were turned in, Katy was brought back to see the doctor.

As soon as she was gone, Ryan asked, "What do you think happened?"

"I don't know," Vince replied. "It doesn't seem like a robbery. There was no cash in her purse, but her credit cards were still in her wallet, and none of her jewelry was taken."

"I agree," Ryan said. "I hate to say it, but it seems clear that what happened to Katy has to be related to the Jackson murder, the Honda, and all that stuff?"

"I was thinking the same thing," Vince said. "That note we found in the Honda links the car to Jackson's murder. Remember, I put Katy's Mt. Pleasant address on that bill of sale I gave to that kid that sold me the Honda. Whoever did this was probably looking for me. That's the only thing I can think of."

Ryan racked his brain, trying to figure out what else might have caused the attack. "Don't take this wrong, but was Katy seeing anyone while you two were separated?"
~~~~

"Not that I know of. Even if she was, I can't see her associating with anyone that would do something like this."

About forty-five minutes later, the doctor walked Katy into the waiting room. Vince immediately stood and went to her. He could see that portions of her hair had been shaved, and good-sized bandages covered the side of her forehead and the back of her head.

The doctor approached Vince and said, "I used about fifteen stitches to close Katy's wounds. Make sure she comes back in seven to ten days to get the sutures taken out. Have her change the dressings every day and keep the wounds dry." He pulled Vince aside. "Katy told me she fell. I'll leave it at that. I wouldn't be surprised if she has a mild concussion. I'd watch her for the next 24 hours, and if she becomes nauseous, starts vomiting, or continues to act confused, get her to a hospital. But what she needs now is rest."

Vince thanked the doctor, paid the deductible portion of the bill, and walked Katy out to the Honda.

"How are you feeling?" he asked.

"I little better."

"All right, no way are you going back to your apartment tonight. You're coming with me back to Ryan's place. The doctor said you need to rest."

They made it back to Ryan's duplex in West Ashley, and Vince helped Katy inside. He gave her one of his Marine T-shirts and said, "You get some sleep. I'll be here."

"I'm sorry, Vince."

"This isn't your fault." Vince again asked her if she had seen who attacked her.

"No, not really, but things are still fuzzy. All I remember is that when I opened the door, I saw the side of a man's face, and he said something before he hit me."

The two boys were in the kitchen when Ryan broached the subject of contacting the police about the attack on Katy.

"Yeah, we need to, but not tonight," Vince admitted. "We'll call them first thin in the morning. But now we all could use some sleep. We'll figure out what to do tomorrow."

CHAPTER 9

ALESSIO HAD FOLLOWED the Honda to Doctor's Care, continuing past the building to a position where he could see the entrance and waited patiently. About an hour later, the woman and two men left the facility and got into the Honda. Alessio followed the car onto I-526, eventually pulling to a stop in front of a duplex apartment just off Glenn McConnell Parkway in West Ashley.

Alessio pulled the Charger forward and watched a woman and two men leave the car and enter the apartment. He slipped on a pair of leather gloves, put on a baseball cap, and waited a good ten minutes before getting out of the Charger. Unable to open the Honda driver's side door, he returned to his car. "Locked."

"You want to pop the lock?" Sammy asked.

"I don't have a Slim Jim," Alessio said, "and even if it did, cars built after the early 2000s have a chip in their ignition system, making it almost impossible to hotwire them. You should know that."

Sammy frowned sheepishly and said, "It's already midnight. What do we do, just sit here?"

Alessio thought for a moment. "I say we call Gino and have him tow it."

Sammy agreed, and Alessio made the call.

The call woke Gino from a sound sleep. He was pissed, but Alessio reminded him that Frank Romano expected his help on this. He quickly agreed and said he'd be there as soon as possible. Realizing there might be security cameras in the area, Gino grabbed a rag to tie around his face and cover his identity. He also used one of his tow trucks that didn't have his company name and replaced the license plate with one he took from a car in his salvage yard.

It was well after one in the morning by the time Gino made it to West Ashley. Alessio was waiting for him down the road from Ryan's duplex.

Gino jumped down from his tow truck, and Alessio pointed toward the Honda. "See that brown Civic? You need to make the hookup quick and get the hell out of here. I'll meet you back at your shop. Mr. Romano wants it crushed along with the Malibu."

At that time of night, the area around Ryan's place was deserted—the only sound was the occasional rustling of tree branches from a gentle night breeze. Gino backed his wrecker into position and had the Honda's undercarriage quickly secured and its front wheels strapped. No one noticed the operation, and he was out of the neighborhood and on his way to Goose Creek in a matter of minutes.

Alessio followed Gino to his shop in Goose Creek. Turning onto Hall Road, the lights illuminating Park's Auto Salvage & Recycling could be seen in the distance. The salvage yard covered almost two and a half acres and was enclosed with a tall metal fence topped with razor wire. Over a hundred cars and trucks were lined up on the grounds, all at different stages of being cannibalized.

Alessio pulled in behind Gino and waited for him to unlock the gate. The office was in a good-sized steel building with three service bays to its right. The yard was lit by halogen spotlights mounted on each corner of the building and one on the large industrial compactor located off to the right of the entryway. Gino opened the gate and waved the Charger through.

He pointed to the Malibu and gave the keys to Alessio. "Go ahead and pull the Malibu behind the Honda."

He then pulled in the wrecker with the Honda in tow next to a large compactor which used a huge descending hydraulically powered plate to crush the vehicles.

Once the Malibu was moved behind the Honda, Gino used what looked like an oversized forklift to pick up the Honda and place it onto the crusher's baseplate. He parked the forklift, walked to the side of the compactor, and engaged the electric motor. The huge upper plate began hydraulically lowering— slowly crushing the Honda until it was unrecognizable. He then used the forklift to remove and stack the remnant of the car next to the other scrap vehicles—all of which would be shipped to one of the major scrap metal processing centers in the state.

Gino scooped up the Malibu, deposited it in the crusher, and flattened it like a pancake.

Ten minutes later, Alessio and Sammy had left Gino's place and were on their way back to Charleston. "We need to call Frank," Alessio said.

"What about that kid and the Honda? What should we tell him?" asked Sammy.

"We tell him everything, and he'll decide what to do." Alessio's call woke up Romano. "Sorry, Mr. Romano, I know it's late."

"Did you get the job done?" Romano asked.

"Yes, sir. But some unexpected things happened."

"Unexpected things?" Romano questioned.

Alessio went on to tell him that the Russo kid had sold the Honda to someone else, and while trying to retrieve it, the kid broke a door down and seriously injured a woman. They finally got the Honda, and Gino crushed it along with the Malibu. "But I'm worried about the kid. He lost his cell phone, and we think it's in the woman's apartment that was hurt."

The phone was quiet for some time before Romano spoke. "This woman, can she identify the kid?"

"Probably, but the man Russo sold the Honda to certainly can. Plus, the kid's phone has his prints on it."

Romano again remained quiet before continuing, "This Russo kid has become a liability. He needs to be removed—as in permanently. Take care of it tonight and call me in the morning."

"Yes, sir," Alessio said, but Romano had already disconnected the call. He put his cell away, turned to look at Sammy, and said, "Frank says the kid's history. We need to take him out tonight, and I assume you have what you need."

Sammy grinned. Like a tailor's tape measure or a doctor's stethoscope—Sammy never went anywhere without his garrot.

~~~~

It was three in the morning by the time they got back to Callaghan's. Alessio parked in front of the bar and told Sammy to get the kid.

"What do I tell him?"

"Just say everything worked out, and we'll drive him home."

Sammy got out of the car and tried the front door, but it was locked. He pounded on the door, and a moment later, a sleepy Eddie Russo appeared from the back of the bar. He opened the front door, still half asleep.

"You lucked out, kid," Sammy said. "We took care of everything, and you're off the hook. Come on, we'll drive you home."

"Great. I was worried you forgot about me."

Russo followed Sammy to the Charger. Sammy got in the back and told the kid to get in the front next to Alessio. Once Russo was inside, Alessio reminded him how lucky he was that they'd fixed the mess he caused.

"I know I screwed up," Russo said. "It won't happen again."
~~~~

Alessio headed down Dorchester, but when he got to the junction of I-526, Russo noticed he headed west and not east.

"Hey, my place is the other way."

"I know," Alessio answered, "I'm going to drop off Sammy first. Just relax."

At this time of night, the freeway was deserted. Alessio glanced at Sammy in the rearview mirror and nodded. Sammy removed the garrote and leaned forward, placing his left foot against the rear backrest for leverage. He threw the wire over Russo's head, pulling back and twisting. Russo reached up to his neck, trying to grab the wire, but it was too late. The wire cut into his neck. Sammy increased the pressure while continuing to pull Russo's head down and back. The kid kicked his legs out, repeatedly pounding the dashboard and destroying the glove compartment. The kicking became less pronounced until about ten to fifteen seconds later, it stopped altogether. Sammy continued to apply pressure for another twenty to thirty seconds. By that time, the garotte wire had cut deeper into Russo's neck. The heart had stopped, the brain died, and all other life functions ceased to exist. Eddie Russo was dead, and a loose end was now tied up.

Sammy looped off the garotte and sat back, breathing heavily. Alessio saw the damaged dashboard and glove compartment and whispered, "Damn it."

Sammy took out Russo's wallet and checked for any forms of identification. He found the $200 Eddie had taken from Katy. He pocketed the bills and then found the necklace.

"Hey, Alessio, look at this. Do you think it's worth anything?"

"Hell, I don't know. Give it to me. I've got a guy who fences jewelry for us. I'll show it to him."

Alessio drove down I-526, turning right onto Savannah Highway, heading toward the Ace Basin National Wildlife Refuge. Approximately 50 miles later, they stopped on the Harriet Tubman Bridge. Alessio and Sammy removed Eddie Russo from the Charger, stripped him naked, and deposited him in the murky waters of the Combahee River. About a quarter-mile down from the bridge was one of the nature preserves protected by the United States Fish and Wildlife Service. This particular preserve was the home of a large population of American Alligators—some of which could grow to over 15 feet in length. It wouldn't take too long for the tide to carry Eddie Russo's carcass to where the alligators would be waiting to welcome him.

The night was beginning to give way to the faint grays of dawn when they made it back to Charleston. Alessio's left a voicemail for Mr. Romano. He kept it brief. "Done."

CHAPTER 10

IT WAS MIDNIGHT before Vince had gotten Katy settled in his room at Ryan's place. He checked on her several times throughout the night, and she seemed to be sleeping soundly.

The following day, he had just left Ryan's place for his morning run when he stopped. He felt a bit confused. He could have sworn he'd parked the Honda in the street right in front of Ryan's Silverado when they got back to the apartment the night before. The Silverado was there, but the Honda was gone. He walked past the truck and surveyed the street, thinking he might have parked in another spot. No luck.

The Honda was gone. But that didn't make any sense. He clearly remembered putting the key on the kitchen counter last night. He jogged back into the apartment, and the key was right where he'd left it. *Where's the Honda?*

He knocked on Ryan's bedroom door. "Ryan, are you up?" He waited and knocked again. "Hey, buddy. Wake up."

He could hear rustling and footsteps. The door partially opened, and Ryan's sleepy face appeared. "What time is it?"

"Almost seven. I need you to get up. We have a problem."

"What?" Ryan said, stifling a yawn.

"The car's gone."

"Wait a minute," Ryan said. "What car are you talking about?"

"The Honda. I just checked, and the Honda is gone."

Ryan was still half in the bag when he said, "Well, where is it?"

"How the hell do I know?" Vince's frustration was evident. "I need you to wake up and get out here."

Ryan opened the door and followed Vince into the kitchen.

Vince picked up the key from the counter and held it in front of Ryan. "Remember when we got back last night? I parked the Honda right in front of your truck."

"Right, I remember," Ryan said.

"So, I'm leaving for my run this morning, and I notice the car was gone. The key is still here, but the car is gone. I'm assuming you didn't move it."

"No, of course not," Ryan replied.

Both guys looked at each other, not knowing quite what to say.

"Maybe that kid you bought it from might have got it," Ryan offered. "If he had another set of keys, he could have stopped by in the middle of the night and driven off with it."

"I doubt it," Vince said. "He never knew where you lived. The only address he had was the one I put on his copy of the bill of sale. That's the Mt. Pleasant apartment where Katy and I lived. I guess he could have followed us back here right after we bought it, but that's a stretch."

"This is crazy," Ryan said. "It doesn't make any sense."

"How about the cops?" Vince queried.

"No way. There are legal parking spaces marked on the street in front of the duplexes."

"Well," Vince said, "all I know is the Honda was here last night, and it's not here now."

~~~~

Ryan had gone back to his bedroom to get dressed, and Vince was making coffee when his cell rang. It was Art Garnett from the Post & Courier. Garnett told Vince he'd come up with a few things concerning Cornell Jackson and wanted to meet later that morning around eleven o'clock.

"That would be fine, sir," Vince said and disconnected the call. When Ryan returned to the kitchen, Vince told him about the call but made it clear that he intended to stay at the apartment with Katy and that Ryan would have to meet with Garnett himself.

"All right, I'll meet him, but what am I supposed to say? We don't have the Honda anymore—much less its title. And I never saved the name of the lady in Columbia that owned it or the license plate number. All we have is the note and a copy of the bill of sale. At least, the bill of sale will have the Honda's VIN number on it."
~~~~

Vince's face fell. "The bill of sale was in the Honda's glove compartment along with the title. Now, all we've got is the note."

The boys were quiet, both coming to the realization that without the car, title, or bill of sale, they had virtually nothing to support a believable story of the stolen Honda and how it could be connected to the murder of Jackson.

Finally, Vince said, "Well, go ahead and meet with Garnett and see what he says. We still need to go to the police, but now we've basically got nothing to back up what actually happened."

~~~~

Ryan made it to the Post & Courier offices at eleven o'clock and was shown to Art Garnett's office.

Garnett met him at his door. "Thanks for coming," He noticed Ryan was by himself. "Where's your friend?"

"I'm sorry, Mr. Garnett. Vince apologizes, but something came up, and he won't be able to join us this morning."

It was clear Garnett wasn't happy.

"Well, I guess we'll have to move ahead without him. Come in and have a seat." Garnett settled behind his desk and continued, "As I understand, your friend, Mr. Kelly, purchased a car from an individual this past weekend. While cleaning the car, a note was found with the name and address of Cornell Jackson on it. It was later discovered that the individual Mr. Kelly bought the car from was not who he purported to be, and both the car and its license plates had been stolen. You later learned that Cornell Jackson was found murdered, and you believe the
~~~~

car, and perhaps the individual who sold it, may have been involved in the murder."

"That's right," Ryan said, "and you were going to check with your sources."

"Correct. I confirmed that a contract was, in fact, taken out on Cornell Jackson. It's common knowledge on the street that Jackson was selling drugs on Michael Coppola's turf. While I can't confirm it, my source is convinced that either Coppola or his second in command, a Jimmy Sanborn, ordered the hit. Coppola would never think of having anyone murdered without first getting approval from Frank Romano. Here's where it gets interesting. The note you found in the car probably links that car to the murder of Jackson. I find it hard to believe that whoever sold your friend that car wasn't also in some way linked to the murderer. And I've got to believe there has to be forensic evidence in the car or on the note and title that could, at least, point the police in the right direction. You need to take everything you have to the police, but before doing that, I need to see the car and its documentation and get some photos for my story. When will your friend be available?"

Ryan had a sinking feeling when he said, "I understand, but some things have happened since we met yesterday." Ryan explained that sometime last night, the Honda disappeared—and with it, the car's title and bill of sale.

Garnett merely stared at Ryan for a moment before saying, "Let me get this straight. You're now telling me you have nothing that would connect anyone or anything to the murder of Jackson. Yesterday you had it, and today you don't."

Ryan pulled out the note and put it on the desk in front of Garnett. "We've got the note."

"That note proves nothing," Garnett replied with a frown. "You can take that to the police, but I'm not sure what they can do without the car and its papers." He stood; his disdain clear. "Too bad this didn't work. I'll walk you out."

~~~~

Ryan arrived back at his apartment by noon.

"How's she doing?"

"Still sleeping," Vince replied. "So, how'd it go with Garnett?"

"Not good," Ryan admitted. He explained how Garnett's sources had confirmed Michael Coppola or his second in command, Jimmy Sanborn, probably ordered the hit on Jackson with the approval of his boss, Frank Romano. "Garnett was excited about everything until I told him the Honda and its paperwork had been stolen. That was it. After that, he basically blew me off. Plus, he said the cops probably wouldn't do much with the note without the car and its paperwork to back it up."

"We still need to take the note to the police and tell them the Honda is gone," Vince said. "But I'm not going anywhere until I'm sure Katy's going to be okay."

"That's fine," Ryan agreed.

"I don't think there's any doubt that whoever did this to Katy are the same people who took the Honda last night," Vince said. "Her address was the only one on the title and bill of sale.
~~~~

Somehow, they must have found out where you lived and got the car. We know the Honda must have been taken some time while we were asleep last night."

"So, if all that's true, where does that leave us?" Ryan asked. "I agree we need to go to the police, but what do we really have? Yeah, we've got the note, but, like Garnett said, that doesn't prove much of anything."

"You're probably right," Vince said, "but we got Katy into this mess. We need to tell her about the Honda, Cornell Jackson, and everything else. And if we go to the police about that stuff, we also need to tell them Katy was attacked. They can get the security camera footage from outside Katy's apartment. Maybe that will show who attacked her. But it's her call whether or not she wants to go to the cops."

Ryan agreed, and they stayed in the apartment until Katy woke up around one o'clock that afternoon. She was still a bit groggy but assured the boys she felt better.

"How about some coffee and something to eat?" Ryan offered.

"Just some orange juice if you have it, thanks."

Ryan poured the juice, and Vince asked Katy to have a seat in the living room. "We've got some things to tell you."

"Okay," she said, settling into the sofa.

Vince told her everything—from buying the Honda, to the note, to Cornell Jackson, to discovering that the car and its documentation were missing that morning.

"We're saying we're sure this was why someone came after you last night," Vince continued. "They were looking for me. We don't have anything to back up our story, but we need to go to the police anyway, and we think you should come with us."

Katy was silent during the five to ten minutes it took for Vince and Ryan to explain everything. As soon as Vince finished suggesting she go to the police, she pointed to her bandages and said, "Someone broke into my apartment and did this to me. Hell, yes, I want to go to the police. Plus, I remember now that someone asked if you were there right before I got hit."

"That fits with why we think it happened," Vince admitted. "We should probably start with the Mt. Pleasant police since that's where you were attacked. Then we can go to the Charleston cops with what happened to the car and the rest of the stuff."

Katy was up off the sofa and on her way to the bedroom. "Give me about ten minutes to put my face on and get dressed." Realizing she wouldn't be going into her real estate office for at least a week, she continued, "I also need to call the office. I only have one closing and two showings this week, but I can get someone to cover for me."

~~~~

They pulled into the Mt. Pleasant Police Station, and after explaining the situation to the desk sergeant, Katy was given some paperwork and told that a detective would be with her shortly. *Shortly* turned into over a half-hour before Detective Joe Wadsworth introduced himself, took the paperwork, and ushered them back to a small conference room. The detective
~~~~

wore a suit and tie. He was of average height and weight; his face was clean-shaven, as was his ebony head. He looked to be in his mid-30s and carried himself in such a way that Vince's first impression was he'd had a military background.

Wadsworth turned on a tape recorder, identified himself, the date, time, individuals present, case number, and subject of the investigation. He eyed Katy's bandages. "I'm assuming those injuries to your head are the result of the break-in, Ms. Pryor. Why don't you tell me what happened?"

"First of all, I'm not sure it was a break-in," Katy responded. "There were two men. One of them seemed surprised when I answered the door. There was a second man that asked me if Vince was in the apartment. When I said no, something hit me, and that's pretty much all I remember."

Vince interrupted, "Even though the cash in Katy's wallet was gone, I agree it probably wasn't a robbery. Nothing else of value was taken."

The detective inquired if she usually carried cash in her wallet.

"I'm in real estate and always keep at least $100 to $200 in cash just in case I have to entertain my clients."

"That's good to know," Wadsworth said. "You indicated there were two men. Could you identify those men?"

"I'm not sure; it all happened so fast. One of them was young, almost like a high school kid. The one that asked me if Vince was there was older. He was also a lot bigger than the younger one."

Detective Wadsworth jotted down a few notes before saying, "That's helpful, but, again, do you think you could identify them if you saw photos?"

"I could try, but I'm not sure."

Wadsworth nodded toward Vince. "And why would someone be looking for Mr. Kelly at your apartment, Ms. Pryor?"

"He's my husband. Well, he was my husband until a few days ago. We just got divorced."

"Interesting," Wadsworth said—his mind searching for how this might affect his investigation.

But before he could continue, Vince said, "That's part of the whole thing. Ryan and I were involved in some things that we think eventually led to Katy being attacked."

"Hold on," the detective said. "And what were those *things you think* led to Ms. Pryor being accosted?"

Vince glanced at Ryan and then back to the detective. "It all started Saturday morning when Ryan and I were looking for a car for me to buy." Vince did his best to recap all the events that happened over the last few days. Ryan broke in a few times giving additional details. It took several minutes to explain the subsequent disappearance of the Honda and its documentation.

"That's quite a story," Wadsworth commented. "So, you're saying all this happened, but there's no way you can prove any of it. Not much for me to go on. And why wasn't the attack reported last night?"

Vince was expecting a reaction like this.

"Look, detective, we know we should have reported it last night, but getting Katy to a doctor was our priority. We're just trying to explain why this thing happened. But it did happen, so what are you going to do about it?"

"Take it easy, Mr. Kelly. I never said we weren't going to follow up on it." Wadsworth pulled out his cell and punched in a number. "Hey, Gene, Wadsworth here. Can you shake loose a tech and camera this afternoon? I've got a breaking and entering with a 10-48." He listened for a moment and said, "Yeah, I know you're backed up. It should only take an hour or so. It's at the Thickett Apartments on Highway 17 across from the Towne Centre Mall. The apartment number is 113." He paused and said, "Yeah, about thirty minutes. You're a good man. I owe you one."

Wadsworth returned his attention to Katy. "One of our forensic techs and I are going to your apartment in about a half-hour. I'm assuming you have a key with you, Ms. Pryor."

"I have one." Katy fished through her purse, removed the apartment key, and gave it to the detective.

"Thank you, I don't imagine we'll be more than an hour or so at your apartment. You are free to go, and I'll call you this afternoon and let you know where we are on this."

"Thank you, detective," Vince said. "What should we do about the Honda, the note, and the rest of the stuff about Cornell Jackson?"

"I suggest you deal with the Charleston Police Department directly on the car. Much of what you told me occurred in their jurisdiction. I'll make a note in my report of everything you told me and what we discover at Ms. Pryor's apartment. I'll make my report available to them if they want it. But to be honest, other than taking a report on a stolen car, I'm not sure what they'll do without actual evidence of a crime being committed in their jurisdiction. All you really have is the note you showed me. Your best bet is to convince them that the note and what happened to you two and Ms. Pryor is related to the Jackson murder case they're investigating. I know they're working the case with the Colleton County's sheriff's office."

"We'll do that," Vince told the detective and asked, "What are you going to do at Katy's apartment?"

"We'll approach Ms. Pryor's apartment as we would in any crime scene. Forensics will check for prints, take pictures, see if there is security footage, and look for clues of what might have happened." He turned to Katy. "I'll let you know when you'll be allowed back in your apartment."

"Wait a minute, are you saying I can't use my own place?"

"That depends on what we find. Hopefully, it won't be long, but it's protocol."

Katy wasn't happy, but at least she had her makeup and a change of clothes.

"I'll need a few more things from you," Wadsworth said. "We're going to have to scan your fingerprints to compare them against any latent prints the tech lifts from the apartment. Follow me, and I'll walk you down to the fingerprinting scanning station and get you started before I leave for the apartment." He gave one of his cards to Katy. "Like I said, I'll call you this afternoon and update you on where we are in the investigation."

When Vince enlisted in the Marines, his fingerprints, face, irises, and DNA data were recorded and sent to the FBI database in West Virginia and the Automated Fingerprint Identification System (AFIS). Ryan's prints were taken and recorded in the AFIS when he got his high school teaching job. Katy had not had occasion for her to be fingerprinted and was biometrically scanned before the three of them left forensics.

Katy and the boys were in the police station parking lot sitting in the truck when Vince said, "Detective Wadsworth said he'd have something for us later this afternoon. I say we hold off seeing the Charleston police until we hear what he has to say. Then we can take what we know downtown and see what they can do about the Honda and the Cornell Jackson note."

CHAPTER 11

WADSWORTH AND THE forensic tech arrived at Katy's place and, after putting on plastic gloves and downing cloth booties, entered her apartment. They immediately noticed the damaged door jamb and the broken security chain. It took about 45 minutes for the tech to take photos, dust for prints, and get samples of the bloodied carpet. They were wrapping up the investigation when Wadsworth spotted a cell phone that was partially hidden under a TV cabinet. The tech took several pictures of the phone where it lay and bagged it. They stopped by the office to see if they could get security tapes on their way out, but it was closed. The detective made a note to follow up on the tapes.

Back at the station, the tech began preparing the fingerprints found at the apartment and the recovered cell phone to be processed through the Automated Fingerprint Identification System (AFIS).

There were only three prints taken from inside the apartment; those were identified as coming from Katy, Vince, and Ryan. The prints from the cell phone were scanned into the system, and it was only a matter of minutes before a match was found. The results were verified by a fingerprint examiner. The prints lifted from the cell phone belonged to an Edward Russel Russo—the last known address being 1327 Kenwood Drive, North Charleston, South Carolina.

Detective Wadsworth had been filling out paperwork when the tech brought him the documentation confirming Russo's prints were found on the phone.

"Bingo!" Wadsworth said. "Good job! This should be enough for an arrest warrant, but I need to know what was on that burner. How fast can you get the computer boys to do their magic?"

"I'll do my best, but I wouldn't hold your breath. Those guys are backed up big time. I figure you're looking at least four or five days before they can even get to it. Plus, from what I heard, this is only a misdemeanor and won't be high on their priorities."

"Well, thanks for your help, and I'd appreciate it if you could do whatever you can do to speed this thing up."

It took Wadsworth about thirty minutes to fill out the arrest warrant request and affidavit, and he was lucky enough to find a judge available to sign it. He advised the North Charleston Police Department of his intent to exercise the warrant within their jurisdiction and left for Russo's Kenwood address, taking two uniformed officers with him.

A North Charleston officer was waiting to observe when they arrived at the address. Wadsworth made the introductions and ordered one of his officers to cover the rear of the house. Accompanied by his own officer and the one from North Charleston, he approached the house and knocked on the front door. It was answered by a woman holding a cigarette and dressed in a sweatshirt and a pair of jeans. She was maybe in her forties, but the deeply lined face and furrowed brow betrayed her actual age. Wadsworth was sure the holes in her jeans weren't a fashion statement. The woman's face showed a combination of annoyance and concern, but she said nothing.

"Excuse me, ma'am," Wadsworth began. "We're looking for an Edward Russo. Does he live here?"

"Yeah, but he ain't here now."

"Do you know where he is?"

"Don't know," she answered. "What's all this about?"

"We just have a few questions for him, ma'am. Do you know when he'll be back?"

"Don't know. Eddie never made it home last night. What kind of trouble has he gotten himself into now?"

"Like I said, ma'am, we just have a few questions. Can you contact him for us?"

"Can't do that. Already tried. He left his phone in his room."

Wadsworth made a mental note to get a warrant to retrieve Russo's regular cell. There was no guarantee the techs could get into it, but it was definitely worth a try.

"Any ideas you have on where he might be?" Wadsworth asked.

"No, but if I had to guess, I'd say he's probably at Callaghan's."

"Callaghan's?" Wadsworth questioned—obviously confused.

"Callaghan's Bar over on Dorchester," she said. "Eddie says he works for the owner, Michael Coppola."

"Thank you, ma'am. May I please get your name and relation to Mr. Russo?" Wadsworth asked.

"Martha Russo. I'm Eddie's aunt. And if you find him, tell him to get his ass home. He promised he'd fix the upstairs toilet."

"We'll do that, ma'am."

CHAPTER 12

IT WAS ONLY a ten-minute drive from the Midland Park to Callaghan's Bar on Dorchester. As soon as the detective and the two uniforms entered the bar, all conversation stopped. It took a moment for their eyes to adjust to the dim light and the thin vale of cigarette smoke hanging in the air like early morning swamp mist. Several customers were seated at the bar, a few more in the booths that lined the right-hand wall, and two men could be seen shooting pool in the back of the bar.

Wadsworth approached the bartender. "I'm looking for Edward Russo. Is he here?"

"Don't know him," the bartender responded.

Wadsworth's eyes scanned the room, coming to rest on the door at the rear of the bar just past the pool table. He started walking toward the entrance to Michael Coppola's office, followed by the two officers.

"Hold on," the bartender called out, "you can't go back there."

Wadsworth grabbed his detective shield from his belt and held it above his head without turning around. The two pool players moved aside, and Wadsworth opened the door. The two officers followed him upstairs. Sanborn was standing in the doorway to Coppola's office, his size blocking the entrance. Wadsworth flashed his badge and brushed past the big man. Amazing what a detective's badge will do.

Coppola was sitting behind his desk and stood when he saw Wadsworth. "Nice of you to knock," his sarcasm evident. "What can I do for you, officer?" Wadsworth ignored Coppola's use of the term officer rather than detective.

"We're looking for Edward Russo. Do you know where he is?"

"No, we don't," Sanborn cut in. "What do you want with Eddie?"

The detective took no notice of the question. "When was the last time you saw him?"

"I don't remember," Coppola answered, "and I suggest you and your two friends leave unless you have a warrant. Have a nice day, officer."

Wadsworth removed the warrant from his jacket pocket. "This is an arrest warrant for Edward Russo. We have evidence that Mr. Russo was present during an assault. If you know where he is and withhold that information, you could be charged with Hindering Prosecution. We were just at Mr. Russo's house in Midland Park. His aunt told us he didn't come home last night and suggested he was most likely here. She also told us Mr. Russo worked for you. Mr. Coppola, I'll ask you again; do you know where we might find Mr. Russo?"

"And I already told you," Coppola raised his voice. "We don't know where he is and haven't seen him for a few days. And Russo does not work for me. That's all I have to say."

Wadsworth took out one of his detective cards, placed it on the desk in front of Coppola, and left the bar.

As soon as the detective and officers left, Coppola turned to Sanborn. "An assault arrest warrant? What was that all about?"

"I told you what Eddie did to that woman. Alessio and Sammy think there's a chance he left a burner phone at her apartment."

"Does anyone know where the kid is?" Coppola asked.

"He ain't been here all day," Sanborn said. "Last time I saw him, he was at the bar last night around ten. Alessio and Sammy were going back to the girl's apartment to see if they could find Eddie's burner. They told the kid to stay at the bar until they got back. That's when I took off and went home."

"You got Alessio or Sammy's cell number?" Coppola asked.

"Yeah, I got Alessio's."

"Call him. See if they know where Eddie is."

Sanborn made the call and listened for a minute before hanging up. He told Coppola that Alessio passed on the information that the Honda was at the girl's apartment when they returned there. She eventually left with two men, and he followed them to an urgent care facility down 17 South. The three finally left the urgent care, and Alessio followed the Honda out to an apartment in West Ashley. He got Gino to tow the car to his salvage yard, where he crushed the Honda and kid's Malibu.

Not wanting anyone else to know Russo was dead, Alessio told Sanborn he dropped him off at his house at 2:00 pm this morning.

"And that's the last time anyone saw him?" Coppola asked.

"I guess so," Sanborn answered. "The funny thing is that cop said Russo never made it home last night. Anyway, I figure Eddie will show up eventually. At least, we know Gino got rid of the Honda. We still got a problem, though. The cops showing up here with a warrant means those two guys and the girl have already been to the police. They'll probably be able to identify Eddie, and that would involve us."

"Hell, Jimmy, we're already involved!" Coppola shot back.

"So, what should we do about it?" Sanborn asked.

"That's up to Mr. Romano. He's already pissed that the Cornell Jackson thing went sideways."

CHAPTER 13

KATY AND THE boys returned to Ryan's apartment and waited patiently for Wadsworth's phone call. It was six that evening and still no call.

"Katy, you have the card Wadsworth gave you, right?" Ryan asked.

"Sure."

"I say we call him," Ryan said. "He should at least be able to tell us what he found at your apartment."

"I agree," Vince offered. "Give me the card, and I'll call."

She did, and Vince made the call. Wadsworth answered, and Vince identified himself. "Katy Pryor is with me along with Ryan Woods. I'll put you on speaker if that's okay."

"That's fine. I was just about to call Ms. Pryor. I have *good news* and *not-so-good news*. The *good news* is that we found a cell phone at Ms. Pryor's apartment. Our techs were able to lift prints from the phone, and when he ran the prints through the AFIS database, we got a hit on Edward Russo, who currently resides in the Midland Park area of North Charleston. Mr. Russo's prints were in the system because he was arrested and served time for petty theft."

"Were you able to find him?" Vince questioned.

"I was just getting to that. We had Russo's prints on the burner phone we found at the crime scene. Because our police station is in the same municipal complex as the city's courts system, I was able to find a judge to sign an arrest warrant. The *not-so-good news* is that when I took some officers with me to apprehend him at his residence, I learned from his aunt that he'd never returned home last night. I also learned that he spent much of his time at a North Charleston bar by the name of Callaghan's. When I visited the bar, I was told he hadn't been there for a while. Michael Coppola, the owner of the bar, said he didn't know Mr. Russo's whereabouts."

"So, what happens now?" Katy asked.

"We'll issue an APB for Mr. Russo advising that he's the subject of an active arrest warrant for assault. We'll also request that the North Charleston Police monitor his home address and the bar he frequents. He may have left town, but we'll eventually find him. However, I have a mugshot of him when he was arrested for theft. Ms. Pryor, I'm going to email you a copy of that photo to see if you can identify him as the individual who attacked you."

"Detective Wadsworth, this is Ryan Woods. I going to give you my email address. We're at my apartment, and I can open the email on my computer. That way, we'll get a better picture of the man."

The detective asked Katy if that was okay with her, and she agreed. He attached the mugshot to the email and sent it to Ryan's internet address. The email appeared in Ryan's inbox a few seconds later. He opened the email and the attachment.

"Jesus!" Vince gasped. "That's him. That's the son-of-a-bitch that sold me the Honda."

"You're right!" Ryan added. "No doubt about it. That's the guy!"

"Ms. Pryor," Wadsworth interrupted, "is the man in the photo the person who attacked you?"

Katy considered the photo before saying, "Maybe, but I'm not sure. It all happened so fast. But doesn't it have to be him if his fingerprints were on that phone?"

"Perhaps," the detective answered, "but the cell phone evidence would be broadly circumstantial without a positive ID. That's not to say he wouldn't be charged—only that there's a good chance he could walk without your positive identification."

"What about my six-grand I paid this guy for the Honda?" Vince was quick to add.

"I don't know about that," Wadsworth said. "From what you told me, the car and its documentation disappeared last night. Even if we find Russo, where's the evidence of the crime?"

"Well, that sucks," Vince muttered. "Where does all this leave us?"

"Like I said, we'll have the APB out on Mr. Russo. When we arrest him, Ms. Pryor will have the opportunity to identify him in a lineup. Hopefully, seeing Mr. Russo in person will help her identify him as her attacker. Regarding your situation with the car, I again suggest you contact the Charleston Police Department as the alleged theft occurred in their jurisdiction."

"We already planned to do that," Vince said.

"Good," Wadsworth said and directed his following comment to Katy. "Ms. Pryor, you told me there were two men the night you were attacked." He quickly referred to his notes. "One was young, and the other man seemed older and bigger."

"Right," Katy said.

Even though Wadsworth was a Mt. Pleasant detective, he was certainly tuned into the various criminal groups active throughout other neighborhoods in the greater Charleston area. The fact that the Russo kid spent time at Callaghan's Bar led him to believe the older man Katy saw that night might be connected to Michael Coppola. Like other mid-level players in the Organization, he also knew Coppola reported directly to Frank Romano.

"I realize you said you're not sure that Mr. Russo was the individual in the photo I just showed you but let me ask you this. If I showed you a series of mugshots, do you think you would be able to identify the other man you saw the night of the attack?"

"Maybe, I just don't know."

"I understand. I would like to have you come down to the station at about one tomorrow afternoon and look at some photos. Would you be willing to do that?"

"Sure."

"Good," Wadsworth said, "We're finished with your apartment, so I can give you your key when I see you tomorrow, and you're free to go back there. You all have a nice evening, and I'll see you tomorrow afternoon."

Once the call was disconnected, Ryan said, "Well, at least we know who the kid is that ripped us off and probably attacked Katy. But based on what the detective said, we're probably not going to be able to do much about either."

"Maybe not," Vince said, "but no way am I letting that kid slide. Let's think this thing through. If that Honda was used in the murder of Jackson, why would someone try to sell it? As soon as I go to the DMV, it will show up as being stolen, if not before."

"You're right," Ryan added, "but the kid didn't seem all that sharp. Maybe Russo was planning on leaving town. I don't know. But we know that his aunt said the kid spends a lot of time at Callaghan's Bar. And that's the same bar Art Garnett said that a mafia guy named Michael Coppola works out of. It makes sense that this Eddie Russo is probably connected in some way to Coppola."

"Boy, you lost me," Katy said. "Sounds way too confusing."

"It does," agreed Vince, "but Ryan's right. It also probably explains why Russo showed up at your apartment. The only address he had for me was the one I put on the Honda's bill of sale. That's the only address I had, so I used our Mt. Pleasant address. I'm sure he thought he'd find the Honda and me there and freaked when you answered the door."

"I agree," Ryan interjected. "But that still doesn't explain who took the Honda from my apartment last night. I would think it's got to be the Russo kid or one of Coppola's people. I bet some of those mugshots Wadsworth wants to show you tomorrow will include Coppola and the guys that work for him."

The three of them were silent for a time, trying to process everything they'd just covered.

Finally, Vince said, "I say we still go see the Charleston police tomorrow morning and report the Honda stolen. I'm not sure what they'll be able to do, but remember Wadsworth told us to push the note we have and how it might be attached to the Jackson murder. Maybe that'll get their attention."

Katy shook her head. "Information overload! I say we go get something to eat."

CHAPTER 14

ALESSIO AND SAMMY entered Callaghan's at 7:30 pm Wednesday night. They walked into Michael Coppola's upstairs office without knocking.

"Mr. Coppola, get your coat," Alessio said. "Mr. Romano wants to see you."

Jimmy Sanborn was in the office and stood—assuming he would leave with his boss.

"Not you," Alessio said. "Only Mr. Coppola."

"That's okay, Jimmy," Michael said. "Stick around, and I'll see you when I get back."

Jimmy Sanborn didn't like the idea of his boss leaving alone with Alessio and Sammy, but he did as he was told.

As soon as Coppola was in Alessio's Charger, he asked what Mr. Romano wanted. Neither Alessio nor Sammy answered him, and they drove in silence a few miles down

Dorchester Road to the empty parking lot of the thrift store that had gone out of business. Alessio parked next to a black Cadillac Escalade and told Coppola that Romano was waiting in the back seat.

Michael slid into the Escalade next to Mr. Romano. As soon as Michael saw Romano's sour face, he knew this would not be a pleasant meeting.

"Michael, you have a nice operation going for you," Romano began. "However, that operation has created a problem for me. I got a call from Chicago this morning. The fact that Cornell Jackson was found concerned Mr. Cataudella and his friends up there. I did my best to reassure Chicago that the situation is under control."

"Frank, I'm sorry all this happened, but Jimmy told me the car and everything was taken care of. I'll handle the Russo kid. He won't be a problem."

"Russo has already been dealt with," Romano replied. "What concerns me are the two men Russo sold the car to and the Mt. Pleasant girl that was hurt."

"Do you want me to do something about them?" Coppola asked.

"No. We have enough heat coming down on us because of the Cornell Jackson thing. We just need to keep our eyes on them. If necessary, my people will deal with them. Now, because you and your people have caused me problems, your monthly payment to the Organization will increase by five percent. Is that understood?"

Coppola was pissed about the increase but knew he had little choice but to agree. "All right, Frank. Is this a permanent thing?"

"It is until I say it isn't," Romano answered. "You can go now."

CHAPTER 15

KATY AND THE boys headed downtown to the Charleston Police Station on Lockwood Boulevard the following morning. Vince informed the desk sergeant he wanted to report a stolen vehicle. He was told someone would be with him shortly.

Ten minutes later, an older uniformed police officer looking to be pushing fifty entered the waiting room. Age lines were beginning to spider around the man's mouth and tired eyes. He approached Vince, Ryan, and Katy with a curt, "Who's Kelly." His expression was as listless as dried paint.

Vince stood. "That would be me, sir."

"This way," the officer said and headed back to what Vince assumed would be an office or conference room.

"Excuse me, sir," Vince said, "but I'd like my friends to come with us. They're also involved in this."

Without turning around, the officer merely waved them on. They entered a large open area divided into several smaller cubbies by six-feet high gray metal dividers. The officer navigated through the maze to the rear of the bullpen area and entered a small conference room.

"Have a seat. I'm Officer Shaw." He nodded toward Katy and Ryan. "Who are your friends?"

"This is Katy Pryor and Ryan Woods. As I said, they both are part of this."

"All right. First off, what's the make, model, and year of the vehicle, and when did you discover it missing?"

Vince passed what information on the Honda—telling Officer Shaw the car was stolen sometime late Tuesday night or early Wednesday morning from in front of his friend Ryan Woods' apartment.

Shaw made some notes and then asked Ryan if his apartment complex had security cameras.

"No, sir," Ryan answered. "I live in half of a duplex, and there aren't any cameras I know of in the area."

"Just a few more questions," Shaw said, "and we'll get the information into our system. Tell me the car's license plate number and VIN."

The officer was poised to copy the information, but when Vince failed to answer, he looked up and again asked, "What's the plate number and VIN?"

"I don't know," Vince replied. "It's kind of a strange situation. That's why I wanted my friends here with me."

Shaw placed his pen down on top of his notepad. "A strange situation? All right, I'll bite. Please explain."

"It's sort of complicated, but it all started last Saturday morning." Vince did his best to explain everything leading up to

Katy being assaulted, Eddie Russo's prints found on a cell phone in Katy's apartment, and the Honda disappearing.

"That's quite a story, Mr. Kelly. You mentioned a note containing Cornell Jackson's name and address on it. Do you have that?"

Vince pulled the note from his pocket, smoothed it out, and gave it to the officer. He examined the note, but it had been crushed and uncrushed so many times that the writing now it was only partially legible. The officer set it aside and asked, "What did your insurance company say when you reported the car stolen?"

It was clear Vince was embarrassed. "I bought it over the weekend and hadn't gotten around to calling them."

"I see," Shaw said—sarcasm evident in his voice. "Too bad about that. I'll tell you what. I'll get what information we have on the car into our system and pass on this note to our detectives handling the Jackson case. Other than that, we'll just have to wait and see if the car shows up." He stood. "We're done here. Follow me, and I'll walk you out."

They were back in the waiting room; Shaw nodded at Vince and left without another word.

They were back in the Silverado when Ryan said, "Tell me if I'm wrong, but was that a waste of time?"

"The detective didn't seem all that interested," Vince said. "But I can't really blame him. I would think being a cop is a lot like what I experienced in the Middle East. It changes you. Face it, not everyone loves the police. Shaw's no spring chicken, and you can imagine what he's seen and had to put up with. Besides all that, we just told him a pretty crazy story, and there's not much for him to work with."

"Maybe so," Ryan said, "but at least what information they have on the car will be in their system. Other than that, I'm afraid we won't get much help from the Charleston police. Maybe it's time we think about forgetting about the whole thing."

Vince was emphatic when he answered, "Hell no! I'm still out six-grand. Plus, Katy had nothing to do with any of this, and look what happened to her."

"Thanks, boys." Katy sarcastically said. "For a minute there, I thought you forgot I was sitting here."

"Sorry, Katy," Ryan said. "So, Vince, I get the feeling I've asked this question before. What do you want to do about it?"

"Let's look at what we know," Vince began. "We know Eddie Russo sold me the Honda, and it's pretty clear he was at Katy's apartment when she was attacked. From what Garnett at the Post & Courier told us, a mafia guy named Michael Coppola works out of a bar called Callaghan's, and that's where Russo hangs out. That's the only real connection we have, right? That is useless unless Katy can ID someone from the mugshots she's going to see this afternoon."

"I suppose so," Ryan answered, "but I can't see us prancing into that bar and accusing Eddie Russo and Michael Coppola of stealing your car and doing a number on Katy."

"Of course not. But that doesn't mean I can't stop by that bar for a beer and see what I can find out."

"Before we do anything," Katy said, "You need to take me to my apartment, so I can get my car."

"You're not thinking about going back there to stay yet, are you?" Ryan asked.

"I don't know. But my car's still there, and I need it. I've got another key to my apartment."

They ate an early lunch at Boxcar Betty's diner on Savannah Highway and tried to hash out their options—even though they were limited. Vince wanted to use Katy's car and stop by Callaghan's Bar that evening to see if he could find out more about Eddie Russo and where he might be.

Both Ryan and Katy were leery about Vince showing up at the bar.

"Hold on there, buddy," Ryan said. "That's a mafia bar, and Coppola might have been the one that ordered the murder of Cornell Jackson. You're just asking for trouble."

"Ryan's right," added Katy. "I'm having second thoughts about all of this. I know you're out the $6,000 you paid that kid. But I'm getting the feeling that maybe we should just back off the whole thing." She pointed to the side of her head. "These people don't mess around. And I agree they're probably involved with what happened to me."

"Listen, Vince," Ryan said, "we've been to both the Mt. Pleasant and Charleston Police Departments, and Katy's seeing Wadsworth again this afternoon. I say let them deal with it."

"And what happens if they don't deal with it?" Vince scoffed. "Sure, they both know about the note, the Russo kid, and what happened to Katy. But what do we have to back up what we say? Yeah, there's the note, but that doesn't prove anything. Trust me, I've been in a hell of a lot more challenging situations than having a beer at that bar. We can deal with all this later. I say the two of us work on cleaning up Katy's apartment this afternoon while she's at the police station."

Both Ryan and Katy were still against Vince going to the bar, but they agreed to set any further discussion aside for the time being.

Earlier that morning, Vince had grabbed a few of Ryan's tools he'd need to fix Katy's door, and the three of them headed out to her apartment. Once she retrieved her car, she could drive to the meeting with Detective Wadsworth while the boys fixed up her place. When Katy unlocked the door to her apartment, it was even more of a mess than they'd left it a few days earlier. In addition to the splintered doorjamb, the blood-stained carpet, and overturned furniture, the remnants of the dark powder used to lift fingerprints could be seen on the interior doors and walls.

"What a disaster," Ryan sighed and thought to himself; *with all the technology out there, you'd think they'd come up with something that wouldn't make such a mess.*

Vince focused on the broken door and asked Ryan for the keys to his truck. "I'll pick up a new security chain and wood molding to fix the door. I'll also get a deadbolt. You can start working on the carpet and the fingerprint stuff the cops used."

Ryan tossed his keys to Vince, and he left for Lowe's to get what he needed to make the repairs. Katy hunted down a bucket and some cleaning supplies for Ryan and was about to go for the police station when she stopped. She was staring at the kitchen counter.

"Ryan, when you and Vince came to my apartment the night I got attacked, did you see a necklace on the kitchen counter next to my purse?"

"No, the only thing I saw was your purse and wallet. I don't remember seeing a necklace, but to be honest, I can't be sure it wasn't there. It was kind of crazy when we got here."

"That's weird," Katy said. "Vince's mom gave it to me the day we got married. I appreciated it, but it was a bit too gaudy for me. It's a family heirloom, and I had it out, so I wouldn't forget to return it to Vince."

"You can check with Detective Wadsworth when you see him," Ryan suggested. "You've got to figure they would have noticed it. Plus, you know they took tons of pictures of the apartment. Do you have a picture of the necklace? If you do, you should give it to Wadsworth."

"I do. There are a few in our wedding album, and the photographer took some pictures when Shelly gave it to me." Katy disappeared into her bedroom and returned a minute later with two photos of the necklace.

She showed them to Ryan. He smiled. "Jesus, Katy. Have you ever worn that thing?"

"No, it's been sitting in my jewelry box ever since I got it. Listen, I have to leave, but I'll call you guys when I finish with Wadsworth."

It was almost three by the time Vince had the door fixed and installed the extra lock. Ryan had the apartment in decent shape—except for the bloodstained carpet, which would need to be replaced.

~~~~

The boys were ready to leave when Vince received the call from Katy saying she'd just left the police station.

"Any luck with Detective Wadsworth?" Vince asked.

"I'll tell you about it later," she replied. "I need to stop by my office. I'll see you back at Ryan's. I got to go." She disconnected the phone before Vince said another word.

Ryan and Vince made it back to the duplex round four that afternoon. Katy showed up an hour later, and as soon as she walked in the door, Vince asked her again about how it went with the detective.

"All right, all right!" Katy impatiently snapped. "Relax. Let me take a breath and sit down?"

Vince smiled and said, "Sure. Make yourself at home. You want a beer?"

"Sounds good, thanks," she answered and returned his smile.

Vince grabbed three beers from the frig, returned to the living room, and gave one to Ryan and Katy. "So, let's have it. How did it go?"

But before Katy could say anything, Ryan asked if she had learned anything about the heirloom necklace. He had already explained to Vince that Katy had left it on the kitchen counter the night she got hurt so she would remember to return it to him.

"I did," Katy answered, "and it was gone. The detective and the tech guy took pictures of the whole apartment, including the
~~~~

kitchen counter. Wadsworth said that whoever took the money probably took the necklace, too. I left the photos with Wadsworth. I'm sorry, Vince, I know how important that was to your mom."

"Don't worry, Katy. As soon as they find Russo, they'll get it back. Now, tell me about the mugshots?"

She took a deep breath and began, "Interesting, to say the least. Detective Wadsworth brought me these big books filled with pictures of men and some women. Kind of like oversized scrapbooks. He told me to take my time looking at the photos. He also gave me a pad of those small yellow sticky notes and asked me to put a note on any page that had a photo of someone that looked even a little like the older guy I saw the night I got hurt. God, I must have gone through over a thousand photos. Some of these guys were gross—I mean like really scary looking."

Vince was losing patience. "We know what mugshot books look like. The question is, did you see anyone that reminded you of the guy?"

Katy frowned and said, "Chill, Vince, I was just getting to that. Don't forget I said I hardly even got a glance at the older man. I'm doing this an hour and must have gone through eight or nine of those big books. Still, I couldn't find anyone that even remotely looked like the guy. It got hard to focus on the pictures. Finally, I turned over one of the pages and froze. It was the old guy! I couldn't believe it. I mean, it was like totally him. I put one of those sticky notes on the page and left the conference room to get Wadsworth. He came back to the room with me, and when

I showed him the picture, he made this weird kind of smile. I had two more of those books, and he told me to finish looking through them."

Now it was Ryan that was growing impatient. "Who was the guy?"

She didn't answer Ryan's question and just continued, "I finished the last two books, but I didn't see anyone else like the man I showed Wadsworth. I asked him who the guy was. I figured it had to be one of Michael Coppola's men with all the stuff you've told me about Eddie Russo and Callaghan's Bar. But get this—he says no. And then tells me the man I picked was one of Mr. Romano's people!"

Vince jumped in and said, "So the Russo kid was with one of Romano's men! I'm not sure I saw that coming. Come on, Katy, what was his name?"

"Alessio Messina," Katy said. "Detective Wadsworth told me he's one of Romano's bodyguards and his most trusted associate. Messina supposedly came to Charleston when the Chicago mafia sent Romano to Charleston to restore their business operations here."

All three of them were quiet for some time, trying to digest how Katy's identification of Alessio Messina might affect them.

Eventually, Ryan said, "This changes things."

"What do you mean?" Katy asked.

"First," Ryan began, "it's clear the only reason you got attacked was that your address was on the bill of sale of that Honda. The Russo kid probably didn't know the car was used in Cornell Jackson's murder, and he screwed up bigtime when he sold it to Vince. The fact that this Messina fellow was with Russo when you got attacked means Romano was probably just as exposed with the hit on Jackson as Michael Coppola was. We always figured Russo or some of Coppola's people took the Honda. Now I'm thinking it might have been stolen by someone working for Mr. Romano."

"Maybe," Vince said, "but whoever took the car has probably already destroyed it. Plus, chances are good that Russo isn't around anymore. If the car and Russo are removed from the picture, then Ryan and I are less of a threat to both Coppola and Romano." Vince shifted his view from Ryan to Katy. "If all that's true, now it's you, Katy, who pose the biggest threat to them because you can identify Alessio Messina."

"That's just fucking great," Katy said. "A few days ago, I'm sitting at my apartment minding my own business, and now I'm in the middle of some mafia murder. Jesus Christ!"

Vince had rarely heard Katy use that kind of language and said, "That's even more of a reason for me to stop by that bar tonight and see what I can find out." Vince genuinely believed he might learn something that would help Katy's situation, but in the back of his mind, he also thought it was an opportunity to discover where Eddie Russo was hiding and get his six-grand back. He remembered what one of his Raider brothers would often say. *If you want to know if the stove is hot, sometimes you have to touch it.*

Even though Ryan and Katy continued to insist that it is was a bad idea, it quickly became apparent that Vince had made up his mind.

CHAPTER 16

THE THREE OF them had a quick dinner before Vince left in Katy's Caprice for the bar. He noticed only four cars were parked in the lot when he arrived—a Lincoln Continental, a Chevy Suburban, a Ford Mustang, and an old Ford Focus. The bar was in an older brick building with a sign above the black steel entry door showing a neon outline of a leprechaun holding a beer mug next to the name Callaghan's. Two small, barred windows sandwiched the main entrance—the one on the left displaying a neon Budweiser sign and the one on the right a Seagram's sign.

Vince entered the bar and took a seat at one of the barstools near the door. He waved at the bartender while his eyes quickly scanned the entire bar. In addition to the bartender, he saw only five other men—four of whom were old geezers probably in their late sixties and seventies. No Eddie Russo. Vince gauged the fifth man sitting in the rear of the bar to be in his mid-to-late-twenties. His long black hair was tied in a ponytail. He wore a black leather vest and a dark gray T-shirt that stretched over massive arms covered with tatts. He was around six feet tall and weighed a good 240—every ounce muscle. The man's eyes hadn't left Vince since he entered the bar.

The bartender eventually left the far end of the bar and approached Vince, who ordered a Bud and a shot of Windsor. The bartender retrieved a bottle of beer from a cooler and poured the shot. "Seven bucks."

Vince removed a ten from his wallet and put it on the bar. Acting as if he had too much to drink, made a mock salute and said, "Keep the change, captain."

The bartender picked up the bill, inserted the ten in the cash register, and pocketed three dollars. He returned to the far end of the bar without saying anything.

Vince downed the shot and took a pull off his beer. He sat for a time before glancing to his right, where an older man sat nursing a beer. Vince swiveled his barstool and leaned across the bar toward the man. In a loud voice, his words intentionally slurred as if he were drunk, he said, "Hey, buddy, I heard a good one yesterday."

The old man cast a sideways glance at Vince, nodded, and returned to his beer.

"So, there were two butt cheeks that walked into a bar. There was a fight going on. One butt cheek says to the other, 'Let's get together and stop this shit.'"

The old man said nothing.

Vince leaned in closer to him. This time his voice was clear and not much louder than a whisper. "Has Eddie Russo been in here today?"

The old man gave a quick shake of his head—his attention remaining focused on the beer resting on the bar in front of him.

A few minutes later, Vince picked up his beer and walked to the rear of the bar—weaving a bit as he went. He inserted two quarters in the pool table's coin receptor and began to rack the balls.

After selecting a pool cue, he smiled at the ponytail man that sat next to what Vince assumed was a door to the bar's office. He was now close enough to judge that the man's muscles resulted from years of lifting weights. Vince knew bodybuilders rarely make good fighters. Although exceptions exist, putting on too much muscle mass is detrimental to the reflexes needed in effective fighting. They might hit hard but generally don't have the stamina or skill to hold their own with someone skilled in street fighting or professional combat. Vince also noticed the man had a tattoo on his right hand—a definite "no-no" if he was ever in the military.

"How about we shoot a game, friend?" Vince asked. "I promise I won't hustle you."

The man remained seated but said nothing, his eyes still focused on Vince.

Vince shrugged his shoulders and proceeded to break the rack. He played for a few minutes, pocketing only two balls before sinking the cue ball. It was apparent he was either drunk as a skunk or a complete rank amateur. Vince shot another rack with much the same results. Eventually, he walked around the table to where the ponytail man sat.

"Hey, bro," Vince said, "you got the time?"

The man pointed to a clock on the wall above the pool cue rack.

It was eight o'clock. "Darn! Where's Eddie? I was supposed to meet him half an hour ago."

The man said nothing.

"Russo, bro. You know Eddie, right?"

The man remained silent.

"Jesus, man, cat got your fricking tongue?" Vince said, his voice growing louder. "Screw it; I need another beer."

As soon as Vince left the pool table for the bar, the ponytail man stood and rapped on the door to Coppola's office. A moment later, Jimmy Sanborn opened the door. "What's up?"

Ponytail pointed toward Vince, who had just got himself another beer and was now weaving his way back toward the pool table. "I get the feeling we might have some trouble with that guy. He seemed pretty shit-faced and was asking about the Russo kid."

"Thanks, Big Mike. I'll take care of it." Sanborn joined the big man, shutting the door leading to Michael Coppola's upstairs office. As soon as Vince made it back to where the two were standing, Sanborn said, "Hello there, sir. Seems like you've had a little too much to drink this evening."

Vince placed the bottle of beer he'd just bought on the side of the pool table.

"Come on, man, this is only my second beer. I feel fine." Vince walked over to where he'd left his pool cue and pointed back to the pool table. "How about you and I shoot a game of pool?"

Sanborn picked up the beer Vince had left on the pool table. "You've had enough for tonight. It's time for you to head home. I can call you a cab."

"I'm not going anywhere. I'm supposed to meet Eddie Russo here."

Two of the old men at the bar got out of their stools and quickly headed for the exit.

Sanborn placed the beer he'd taken from Vince on the table behind him, stood up straight, and took a step toward Vince. He had several inches and a good 60 pounds on Vince. "Like I said, we'll get you a cab, but you *are* going to leave."

Vince pointed to the bottle of beer on the table behind Sanborn. "I just bought that beer."

Sanborn took out his wallet, removed a five, and placed it on the pool table next to Vince. "That should cover the beer. I suggest you pick it up and leave quietly." Sanborn nodded toward his bouncer. "Or I'll ask Big Mike here to help you leave. And trust me, that's not something you want to deal with."

Vince took a step back and leaned against the pool table. He looked at the five-dollar bill next to him but made no attempt to pick it up. "Where can I find Eddie Russo?" This time Vince's voice was crystal clear. "Tell me where he is, and I'm out of here. No harm, no foul."

Sanborn shook his head and sighed. He turned to Big Mike. "Go ahead and see the gentleman out."

The big man took a step forward, roughly grabbed Vince's right elbow, and said, "Let's go, pal."

Vince moved his right foot in front of Mike's left leg, suddenly bent down, and thrust his right arm forward, causing him to stumble slightly and lose his grip. Big Mike quickly righted himself, smiled, and said, "So that's how you want to play it."

Moving surprisingly fast, Big Mike drove his shoulder into Vince's chest, slamming him into the side of the pool table. He took a quick step back and threw a right cross directed at Vince's jaw. Vince ducked, quickly shifting his head to the left, causing Big Mike's fist to merely graze his forehead. At the same time, Vince's right hand shot forward, his front two knuckles connecting directly to the big man's throat, disabling his larynx. As if in the same motion, Vince pivoted to his left until he was in a position to use the side of his right hand to strike Mike's carotid artery area with just enough force to the vagus nerve to cause an interruption in the heart's ability to pump blood resulting in dizziness and a brief loss of consciousness. Jimmy Sanborn watched Big Mike's knees crumble, and he tumbled face-first to the floor like a house of cards. Everyone has a plan until they get punched.

Sanborn was stunned by the speed and efficiency this seemingly drunk person had disposed of one of his toughest men. He cautiously approached Vince and said, "All right, you've made your point, but, like I said, you're still going to have to go one way or the other."

"Like I said, I'll leave when you tell me where Eddie Russo is, and I'm gone like I was never here."

"And what is it you want with Eddie?" Sanborn asked.

"He owes me money."

"I'm sorry to hear that, but that's between you and him." Sanborn's eyes surveyed the bar. "As you can see, Eddie isn't here. As a matter of fact, I haven't seen him for a while."

At that point, the door behind Sanborn opened, and Michael Coppola appeared. He saw Mike sprawled out on the floor.

He glanced at Sanborn. "What the hell's going on?"

His eyes still riveted on Vince, Sanborn said, "This fellow is looking for Eddie. Says he owes him money for a car. Says he won't leave until he finds out where the kid is."

Vince smiled. "I don't seem to remember saying anything about a car."

Coppola's gaze returned to Big Mike for a second and then settled on Vince. "How much does Eddie owe you?"

"Six-grand."

"What for?" Coppola asked.

Not wanting to say more than he already had, Vince merely repeated, "I said he owes me six-grand. That's all."

Sanborn had several inches and 60 pounds on Vince. He took another step closer to Vince and said, "I'll handle this, Michael?"

"No," Coppola answered and stared at Vince for a time before continuing, "I'm sorry Eddie owes you money, but, as you can see, he isn't here, and I have no idea where he is."

Vince was about to say something when he heard the unmistakable sound of a pistol being cocked and felt its cold steel barrel against the back of his head.

"Be a good boy, now," the bartender said. "Hands up—nice and easy. I shoot you; I gotta clean up the mess."

Vince slowly raised both hands in front of him, never taking his eye off Coppola. "If you see Eddie Russo, tell him I intend to get my money."

"I hope you get it back, but now it's time for you to disappear—one way or the other."

The bartender backed away; his gun still leveled at the back of Vince's head.

Vince smiled, slowly turned, and casually walked out of the bar.

As soon as Vince shut the door behind him, Coppola ordered Sanborn to help Mike—who was trying, without much luck, to stand. "So that's the guy Eddie sold the car to," Coppola said. "That's the first time I saw anyone take Big Mike down. This whole thing is turning into a real shit show."

By this time, Sanborn had gotten Mike up and had him sitting on a chair. He was still clutching his throat—his breathing intermittent and labored.

"So, what do we to do about it, boss?" Sanborn asked.

"I don't know—too many loose ends. First, the cops show up here with a warrant for Eddie. Now we got some badass who wants Eddie to give him his money back. And where the hell is Eddie, anyway?"

Sanborn thought for a moment. "Remember last year when Bennie Franco was drunk and got into a tussle with an off-duty Charleston cop—beat him up bad. Romano sent Bennie off to Atlanta until the whole thing cooled down. I bet that's what he did with Eddie."

"Possibly," agreed Coppola.

"Maybe the guy that showed up tonight will go away if we give him the six-grand," Sanborn said.

"No!" Coppola quickly answered. "We do that, and we're automatically linked to the Honda, and maybe to the Jackson hit."

"Wait a minute," Sanborn said, "Gino already got rid of the Honda."

"I know that! But what happens if the cops find and arrest the kid? Plus, it doesn't mean the girl won't identify Eddie as the one that hurt her, or the guy that just left won't identify the kid as the one who sold him the Honda. If that happens, we're screwed. I'm already on thin ice with Romano. As much as I hate to do it, we need to let Frank know about the guy who was just here."

~~~~

It was approaching nine that night by the time Vince got back to Ryan's apartment. He hadn't even shut the door before Ryan asked, "So, what happened?"

Vince gave Ryan and Katy a brief description of what transpired at Callaghan's, leaving out any mention of his run-in
~~~~

with Big Mike or the bartender's gun to the back of his head. "I met Michael Coppola and two of his main guys. There's no doubt they know Russo sold me the Honda."

"How about Russo? Did you see him?" Katy asked.

"No. And I got the feeling the kid hasn't been around there for a while."

"I bet he left town," Ryan said. "Probably planned on doing that all along."

Knowing how stubborn Vince could be, Katy said, "You did your thing tonight, Vince. Now, will you let the police do their job?"

Vince turned slightly away from Katy—a mulish smile materialized, and he said, "Sure. We'll see what happens."

"Oh, no, Vince," Katy sighed, having seen that smile all too often.

CHAPTER 17

FRANK ROMANO AGREED to meet Coppola at noon on Friday. The meeting was to be held at Gennaro's Restaurant on Sam Rittenberg Boulevard. The restaurant normally didn't open until 4:00 p.m.; however, the owner, Sal Rogelio, made exceptions for Mr. Romano.

Coppola and Sanborn arrived early and were met by Rogelio. "Gentlemen, Mr. Romano should be here shortly." In an apologetic tone, Rogelio turned to Sanborn and told Jimmy that Mr. Romano had requested that only Mr. Coppola be present for their luncheon. "I have a table set up for you in the front." He snapped his fingers, signaling one of his waiters to escort Jimmy to the table that had been arranged for him.

Rogelio led Michael to a private room in the rear of the restaurant. He ordered his waiter to pour some water and take his drink order. Coppola declined the waiter's suggestion of a glass of Antinori Chianti Classico, 2015—opting instead for coffee.

Frank Romano, along with Alessio and Sammy, arrived a short time later. Sammy remained by the restaurant's front door while Rogelio led Mr. Romano and Alessio to the private dining room. Alessio took up a position by the entrance to the room.

As soon as Romano was seated, the waiter poured him a glass of sparkling water and delivered two porcelain serving plates and a platter of antipasto.

Romano gestured to the antipasto. "Please enjoy. Sal makes the best antipasto this side of Italy."

The two men served themselves, and Coppola said, "Thanks for meeting me, Frank. I wanted to discuss the situation with Eddie Russo and let you know about something that happened at my bar last night."

"That's fine, Michael, but let's not let business spoil Sal's antipasto. We eat first, then we talk."

For the next twenty minutes, they ate, sharing little conversation. Finally, Romano waved to the waiter, who removed the plates and empty platter. "Now, Michael, let's hear what you have to say."

"Thank you, Frank. I know you told me Eddie Russo has been dealt with. It's been several days since I've seen him, and I wondered what you meant by 'dealt with.' I know the police have issued an assault warrant for him, and I'm concerned what he might say if he's arrested."

Romano casually removed his napkin, folded it, and placed it neatly on the table in front of him. He straightened the lapels on his suit jacket before acknowledging Coppola. "I understand your concern, Michael. Russo won't be a problem in the future. I said he has been dealt with, and that's all you need to know."

It now became clear to Coppola what Romano meant by Russo being dealt with. He felt a wave of remorse wash over him because he'd always intended to protect Eddie as a posthumous promise to his good friend, Pete Russo. But he also knew better than to question Romano further.

"You mentioned something that happened last night at your bar," Romano inquired. "Tell me about it."

"Sure. This fella shows up at the bar last night and starts causing trouble, so Jimmy tells Big Mike to get rid of his ass. You know Mike, right?"

"I know him."

"Yeah. So, Jimmy tells me Mike makes a move on the guy, and a second later, Mike's on the floor unconscious. Nobody's ever done that to Big Mike before."

Romano glanced at his watch and leaned forward. "Michael, you didn't want a meeting just to tell me one of your boys got his ass kicked. What is it?"

"The guy was looking for Eddie Russo. He said Russo owed him six-grand. He's got to be the guy Eddie sold the Honda to. I know Gino got rid of the car, but I still feel like this guy's going to be a problem. Plus, we know another person was with him when Russo sold him the car. You got to figure both of them will be able to connect Russo to the car."

"I already know that." Romano was clearly losing patience with Coppola. "And I also know about the arrest warrant for Russo. It doesn't take a genius to figure the cops have already connected you and your boys to the Cornell Jackson hit. But without Russo and the Honda, they can't prove anything. So, we do nothing with the guy that showed up last night or his friend. Is that understood?"

"Sure, Frank. But what happens if that guy comes back to the bar?"

"Christ, what did I just tell you? Just act like you don't know shit about shit. If he becomes more of a problem, let me know, and I'll deal with it. I don't want you or your people involved." Romano stood—the meeting was over. "Now, go make me some money."

CHAPTER 18

VINCE AND KATY had a rather heated argument Friday morning concerning her insistence on returning to her apartment. Their matching stubborn streaks contributed to their divorce.

Vince would move into the Grand Oaks apartment in about a month, and he and Ryan had spent a few hours earlier that afternoon hunting down a bed and some furniture for the place.

Vince hadn't said much the entire afternoon, and Ryan asked what was bothering him.

"I'm all right. Just a little pissed that Katy's going back to her apartment. I still don't think it's safe."

"You're probably right, but it's her decision. And in case you don't remember, you two aren't married anymore. Let's get back to the apartment. You need to sign-up on Indeed or ZipRecruiter and start looking for a job. Which reminds me, you're going to still need a car."

"I know that!" Vince said, his frustration showing. "The question is: How am I going to afford one? I told you I only had $15,000 after the divorce. The six-grand for the Honda is gone, and I just spent $2,000 on furniture. Plus, I've still got four more months of Katy's rent to pay. If I don't get that six-grand back from that kid, no way can I buy one."

"I can help out," Ryan offered.

"No! You've already done enough. I'll figure something out."

"What about your mom?" Ryan asked. "Could she kick in some cash?"

"No way," Vince answered. "She can barely cover her own expenses."

"You can go to a dealership and make payments," Ryan offered.

"Yeah, but the last time I checked, that's tough to do without a job. I said I'll figure it out."

Vince spent the balance of the afternoon and well into the evening creating a resume and submitting cover letters for possible job opportunities. He also signed up with an organization called MilitaryHire, which placed veterans with Fortune 500 companies. Finally, Ryan dragged him away from his computer and convinced him to go out and get something to eat.

They stopped in the Stones Throw Tavern just off Glenn McConnell Parkway. The place was crowded, but they found a table in the back. Ryan was studying the menu when Vince said,

"I figure Eddie Russo has either left town or is in hiding somewhere."

"I think you're right, and I also know what you're thinking," Ryan said. "You think if you can't find Russo, you'll get your money back from that Coppola guy. Am I right, or what? Christ, Vince, can't you just accept that the money is history and move on? Remember what Art Garnett said. Coppola is part of organized crime."

"Spiritus Invictus." Vince said.

"Spiritus what?" Ryan asked.

Vince smiled. "The Raiders. Spiritus Invictus. That's our motto. '*Never quit. Never surrender. Never fail. Adapt to the situation. Gain and maintain the initiative.*'"

"Jesus, Vince. You're not in Afghanistan anymore." Ryan waved his hand around the bar. "This is Charleston, South Carolina!"

Vince smiled again and simply repeated, "Spiritus Invictus."

"I knew it," moaned Ryan. "You're going to do it, aren't you?"

Before Ryan could say anything else, the waiter brought the beers and took their food orders. As soon as he left, Vince said, "Don't worry, buddy. I'm not going to do anything stupid. Relax and drink your beer."

They managed to finish their meal without further talk about Eddie Russo, Michael Coppola, or the lost $6,000.

~~~~
~~~~

Vince was up bright and early Saturday morning, and after finishing his regular five-mile run, he logged into his computer. He was surprised to find three responses from his previous day's job searches. One was from a private security company specializing in installing and monitoring high-end corporate security systems. The second was a response for a logistic technician for a nationally known trucking corporation. The final answer came from a company advertising for a telecommunication consultant at AT&T, but that one turned out to be a sales clerk at one of their retail stores. The first two seemed to be decent possibilities, and Vince was in the process of researching them when Ryan showed up in the kitchen hunting for coffee.

Ryan pointed to Vince's computer. "What are you up to?"

Vince explained about the job search responses he'd received, and they spent the next half-hour discussing the pros and cons of each opportunity. After declining the AT&T offer, he spent the next hour completing the questionnaires that would be required before scheduling an initial Zoom interview.

Vince felt good about the job possibilities, and his morning got even better when his mother called asking him to have lunch with her. He said he'd call her right back. Ryan had his regular Saturday afternoon pick-up basketball game at St. Andrew's Park and told Vince to take his truck to meet his mom. He would have one of his buddies pick him up. The guys usually stopped for a beer and something to eat after they finished playing. He told Vince not to worry when he got the truck back. Vince thanked him, called his mom, and agreed to meet her at Five Loaves Café in Mt. Pleasant at noon.

As usual, Ryan's mom, Shelly, had arrived early and was already seated with an iced tea in front of her when Vince showed up at the restaurant. "Hi, baby," Shelly said, "give your mama a hug."

Vince obliged his mom with a hug and kiss on the cheek. He sat down, waved the waitress over, and asked for iced tea. "You look good, Mom."

"The hell I do," she answered, "but bless you for saying that. I heard you're staying with Ryan."

"Right, but I just signed a lease for an apartment in West Ashley. I'll be moving in in a month or so." Vince described where it was located and what it was like. He also talked about the furniture he'd just bought and the good news on the job front.

"So, sweetheart, tell me about Katy. I still can't believe it."

"We'll be fine, Mom. Don't worry. She said she'd call you and stop by. Really, it going to work out. We're good friends, and she still means a lot to me."

They ate their lunch, talking about all the things they usually talked about—her job at the county library and her pesky neighbors.

Plates and glasses were removed, and when the waitress brought the check, Shelly grabbed it.

"Come on, Mom. Let me get that."

"Hush up," Shelly replied, and after perusing the check, she took the money from her purse and placed it on the table. Her countenance took on a serious cast. "There's something else I need to talk to you about."

"Don't tell me you're dating," Vince said with a smile.

"Don't be silly. This is serious."

"Sorry, Mom. Go ahead."

Shelly took a deep breath and explained that his dad, George Kelly, was released from the Goodman Correctional Facility in Columbia two months ago. He'd served six months of a twelve-month sentence for aggravated second-degree assault.

"Jesus, Mom, why didn't you tell me this before?"

"I'm sorry, dear," Shelly replied. "You were overseas, and I didn't want to worry you with something like this."

"Second-degree assault?" Vince questioned.

"I don't know the details," Shelly said. "I just know he beat up someone pretty bad. I know you and your dad haven't talked in a long time. I don't have anything to do with him either. I just thought you should know."

Vince was quiet for a moment before saying, "Assault? I can't say I'm all that surprised. We both know about his temper. Plus, I remember you telling me about the kind of people he was hanging around with. Who knows what he got himself into?"

Shelly reached across the table and took hold of Vince's hand. "I'm sorry about all this, dear. I just thought you should know."

"Don't apologize for him," Vince said. "I'm sure he got what he deserved. And let's face it; we both knew something like this was bound to happen."

"Maybe so," Shelly said, "but enough of that. Now, you know I've got plenty of stuff I'm not using, so please come over to the house and take what you need for your apartment."

"That's nice," Vince said and stood to leave. "I'll stop by tomorrow and see what you've got."

Vince said goodbye to his mom and was in the parking lot sitting in the Silverado and thinking about his dad. George Kelly had never been an openly emotional person, especially after retiring from the Marines. He'd show up for Vince's high school football games but never to teacher conferences and other school activities. Vince wouldn't admit that his father's distance and seemingly disinterest hurt him in high school. He'd been envious of Ryan's relationship with his parents—one of the reasons he spent so much time at the Woods' house back in his teen years. His time in the Marines had solidified his self-esteem and allowed him to view his father's flaws with a bit more objectivity.

It was still early afternoon, and he knew Ryan's round-ball game wouldn't start until two. He put the truck into gear and thought to himself, *Time to do some recon.*

Twenty minutes later, he pulled into the industrial park and drove slowly past AC Global Imports. It was a small building located at the end of a cul-de-sac with a few parking spaces in front. There was a warehouse and a single loading bay in the rear. Security cameras were mounted on all four corners of the building. After appraising the structure and taking in the surrounding, he left for Callaghan's Bar.

Fifteen minutes later, he parked the Silverado across the street from Callaghan's. An old two-story apartment building was located directly across from the bar and flanked by the apartment's small parking lot. An empty store that had been a check-cashing business was located next to the apartment's parking lot. He could see no evidence of security cameras on the apartment building. From his vantage point, he saw two cameras mounted on the front of Callaghan's—one focused on the main entry and the other covering the parking lot to the right of the building.

There were only two cars parked in the lot. One was an older Ford Focus and the other a small Hyundai Accent. Vince remembered the Ford Focus from when he was at Callaghan's. That night there had also been a Continental, a Suburban, and a Mustang. He assumed the Continental, Suburban, and Mustang probably belonged to Coppola, Sanborn, and Big Mike, respectively. It seemed apparent that the Focus was likely owned by the bartender and that Coppola, Sanborn, and Big Mike were not currently in the bar.

To the left of the bar was a parking lot for a small beauty salon—the kind where older, silver-haired women sat under those old hair-drying hoods reading magazines. Two security cameras covered the salon's parking lot. Vince's first reaction was that the cameras were fake because the unit had no visible wiring. He took a photo of the camera, allowing him to search the internet later to determine whether the specific brand was legitimate or a knockoff.

Despite the building itself being old, Vince gauged it to be relatively secure. His eyes focused on the heavy steel front door and the iron bars on the front two windows. He had not seen the back of the building but was sure fire regulations would require at least one rear exit.

It was still early afternoon, and he knew Ryan's round-ball game wouldn't start until two. He put the truck into gear and thought to himself, *Time to do some recon.*

Twenty minutes later, he pulled into the industrial park and drove slowly past AC Global Imports. It was a small building located at the end of a cul-de-sac with a few parking spaces in front. There was a warehouse and a single loading bay in the rear. Security cameras were mounted on all four corners of the building. After appraising the structure and taking in the surrounding, he left for Callahan's Bar.

He parked the Silverado across the street from Callaghan's twenty minutes later. An old two-story apartment building was located directly across from the bar and flanked by the apartment's small parking lot. An empty store that had been a check-cashing business was located next to the apartment's parking lot. He could see no evidence of security cameras on the apartment building. From his vantage point, he saw two cameras mounted on the front of Callaghan's—one focused on the main entry and the other covering the parking lot to the right of the building.

There were only two cars parked in the lot. One was an older Ford Focus and the other a small Hyundai Accent. Vince remembered the Ford Focus from when he was at Callaghan's.

That night there had also been a Continental, a Suburban, and a Mustang. He assumed the Continental, Suburban, and Mustang probably belonged to Coppola, Sanborn, and Big Mike, respectfully. It seemed apparent that the Focus was likely owned by the bartender and that Coppola, Sanborn, and Big Mike were not currently in the bar.

To the left of the bar was a parking lot for a small beauty salon—the kind where older, silver-haired women sat under those old hair-drying hoods reading magazines. Two security cameras covered the salon's parking lot. Vince's first reaction was that the camera was fake because the unit had no visible wiring. He took a photo of the camera, allowing him to search the internet later to determine whether the specific brand was legitimate or a knockoff.

Despite the building itself being old, Vince gauged it to be relatively secure. His eyes focused on the heavy steel front door and the iron bars on the front two windows.

Vince left the Silverado, crossed the street, and approached the bar by walking through the salon's parking lot. He moved around to the rear of the building and confirmed there was, in fact, a rear entrance with a security camera mounted above it.

Time to shake things up, he thought.

He returned to the front of the bar and entered. It took a moment for his eyes to adjust to the shadowy surroundings. As soon as he got his bearings, he noticed the bartender sitting at the far end of the bar talking to one of the old men he'd remember from the other night. No one else was in the bar. Vince took a seat at the bar close to the door, smiled at the bartender, and gave him a mock salute. The bartender remained seated at the end of the bar, making no effort to move or even acknowledge Vince. Vince got off his barstool, moved down the bar, and sat a few stools from the old man and bartender.

"How about a Bud, my friend?" Vince asked.

Without leaving his seat, the bartender said, "Just ran out of Bud."

"You got Miller Lite?" Vince asked.

"Out of that, too." The tender answered.

"Wow! Must have been a run on beer around here." Vince reached behind him and pulled out his wallet. He counted out three twenties and placed them on the bar in front of him. "Just tell me where I can find Eddie Russo, and I was never here."

The bartender stood, walked to the cooler, and grabbed a bottle of Miller Lite. He put the beer on the bar in front of Vince and picked up the bills. "Don't know an Eddie Russo. But thanks for the tip." He put the bills in his pocket, returned to the end of the bar, and picked up his cell phone.

The bartender was about to dial when Vince picked up the Miller Lite, chugged it, and placed it gently back on the bar. He smiled at the bartender, gave him another salute, and said, "Thanks for the beer. Taste great, less filling! Oh, and give my regards to Mr. Coppola."

As soon as Vince left the bar, the bartender called Michael Coppola.

~~~~
~~~~

Vince was about to leave Callaghan's when he received two more responses from his Indeed account. The first was for a Direct TV installation technician, which he immediately declined. However, the second response piqued his interest. It was from the Homeland Security's U.S. Customs and Border Protection Department. The position was for a Maritime Interdiction Agent based in Charleston. He drove back to the apartment and spent forty-five minutes completing the necessary preliminary forms to apply for the position.

Vince figured he had enough time to swing by St. Andrew's Park and watch Ryan play ball. He arrived at the park in time to catch the last two games. The guys finished playing around four, and Ryan and Vince joined several other players at Mueller's Pub. It was an eclectic group of guys—most in their twenties and thirties with a few much older men. Some of the younger players had gone to high school with Vince and peppered him with questions about his time in the Marines.

Ryan finally pulled Vince aside and asked, "So, how'd your lunch go with your mom?"

"Interesting," he replied and went on to tell Ryan about his father's incarceration for assault.

"Assault? Jesus, Vince. You said he got out two months ago. What's he doing now?"

"Don't know, don't care," Vince answered. "Don't have the time or desire to deal with him. Mom feels the same way." Vince had no inclination to talk about his dad and quickly changed the subject by telling Ryan about the latest job response for the interdiction agent.

"Wow!" Ryan said. "That sounds like the best one yet."

Before Vince could answer, another one of his buddies from high school slapped him on the back and said, "Damn, boy, look at you!" Vince brought his friend up to date on his time in the military without sharing many specifics.

For the next hour, the group reminisced with the help of a few more rounds of beer until Vince tossed the keys to Ryan and said, "Let's go, buddy."

Ryan tossed them right back and said, "You've only had a beer or two. Congratulations, you are now designated as the designated driver."

About six that evening, Vince suggested they go out for a bite to eat, but Ryan declined—citing a combination of the beer buzz and the lingering endorphin high from two hours of full-court basketball. A pizza was ordered, and the two spent an uneventful evening watching ESPN.

~~~~

Coppola had just disconnected his cell phone and turned to Sanborn. "That was Frank. He was tending bar this afternoon when that Kelly guy showed up."

"The guy's got a lot of nerve. I'll give him that," Sanborn added, "but I feel he's not going away, and he's hell-bent on finding Eddie."

Coppola was convinced Eddie Russo was dead but saw no reason to tell Sanborn.
~~~~

"I ain't worried about Eddie," Coppola said. "What I am worried about is if this Kelly guy keeps pushing, it's bound to kick up more dust on the Cornell Jackson thing. Eddie ripped him off, and we know he's already gone to the cops."

"So, what do we do?" Sanborn asked.

"As much as I hate to say it," Coppola replied, "we need to let Romano know this Kelly guy ain't backing off. Frank made it clear his people will deal with Kelly if it comes to that."

"He'll be pissed," Sanborn said.

"I know he'll be fucking pissed! But it'll be worse if we say nothing, and the guy manages to bring the cops deeper into the thing." Coppola was flustered but reached for his phone and called Frank Romano.

It didn't go well. Romano had just about had it with Coppola. Granted, he had agreed to let Michael handle the hit on Jackson, and while the gray-haired man would not have been Frank's choice, he'd heard positive things about the man. The hit went bad, and Coppola's jackass kid made it worse by failing to get rid of the car used in the murder. That gave Romano no choice but to remove Eddie Russo from the equation. And even though Gino Vitale had gotten rid of the Honda, this Kelly guy seemed to be hell-bent on finding Eddie Russo and getting his money back.

Romano hung up the phone. His head made a slight assenting movement, and he turned to Alessio. "You've got the phone number for this Vince Kelly fellow and the address where Gino picked up that Honda, right?"

"Yeah, his phone number was on that bill of sale Eddie gave me, and I remember the place where Gino towed the car from. It was out in West Ashley off Glenn McConnell Parkway."

"Good, I need you and Sammy to take care of something for me."

CHAPTER 19

SUNDAY WAS A laid-back day for both Ryan and Vince.

They drove out to Mt. Pleasant Sunday afternoon together. Ryan was having an early dinner with his mom and dad and let Vince use his truck to rummage through some of his mom's things he may be able to use in his new apartment. He loaded the truck with things his mom insisted he would need. Vince and his mom ate a quick dinner before he swung by Ryan's parents' house to pick him up.

When Vince pulled back into the driveway, Ryan doubled over in laughter.

The bed of his Silverado was filled with boxes of towels, sheets, tables, lamps, dishes, silverware, pots and pans, and other kitchen and household items.

"Did you leave anything for your mom?" Ryan joked.

"You wouldn't believe all the stuff she's kept over the years. Plus, I never realized all the things I was going to need. Katy did most of the organizing. Hell, I'm used to living out of a duffle bag!"

Ryan was peering into one of the boxes in the bed of his truck when he spotted a Brittany Spears poster. He unrolled it, smiled, and said, "Did someone have a crush on Brittany?"

"Jesus, Ryan, I was eleven when I got that," Vince said with a sheepish grin.

Ryan pulled out an old, ragged cloth monkey doll. He held it up and asked, "And who's this little fellow?"

"That's Mr. Monkey," Vince replied. "Mom said she gave it to me when I was about two."

Again, Ryan couldn't resist another good-natured jab at his best friend. "Well now, isn't that special. Anyway, what do we do with all this?"

"We should be able to fit everything in the storage unit I rented. At least until I move into the new place."

"Works for me," Ryan said.

It only took them about twenty minutes to transfer the items from the truck to the storage unit.

As they were finishing, Ryan saw a four-to-five-foot, heavy-duty metal cabinet in the back of the unit. The cabinet was secured with a laminated steel padlock.

Ryan pointed at the cabinet and asked, "What's in there?"

"Just some old military stuff," Vince replied quickly. "Let's get out of here. I'm whipped." It was clear Vince did not want to get into what was in the cabinet.

"Really, what's in the cabinet?" Ryan persisted.

"Just photos and memorabilia from my time in the Marines. I'll show you sometime. Come on. I could use a cold one about now."

They were back at the apartment by 8:30. After a few beers, they called it a night and headed off to their bedrooms—both fast asleep by ten that night.

<p style="text-align:center">~~~~</p>

It was three o'clock Monday morning, and the street in front of Ryan's apartment was deserted as a cemetery at midnight—less the ghosts.

"How do you want to handle this?" Sammy asked.

"You've got your knife, right?" Alessio asked.

Sammy removed a switchblade from his pocket and flipped open its eight-inch blade—illegal in South Carolina.

"Good," Alessio said when he saw the knife. "I'm going to drive a few houses past the place before letting you out. Make sure you've got the ski mask on. Just puncture one of the truck's rear tires. That's all Mr. Romano wants done. Make it quick. I'll turn around and pick you up where I dropped you off. Got it?"

Sammy nodded and pulled the mask down, covering his face.

Alessio stopped the Charger several houses beyond Ryan's duplex, and Sammy jumped out. He bent down and jogged through several front lawns until he arrived at the duplex. A quick jab of the knife into the sidewall of one of the Silverado's rear tires gave off a fairly loud "pop" followed by a steady "hiss" as the tire slowly flattened. He was back in the Charger seconds later.

Within minutes, they were headed east on I-526.

"Take out the burner and send the text," Alessio ordered.

~~~~

Vince was up early Monday morning. He had his running shorts and T-Shirt on and had just put his earbuds in when he noticed the text. It was from a number he didn't recognize. He opened it and was initially confused.

The text read, "Back off, tough guy."

Then it hit him. *Got to be Coppola. Hell. Maybe even Romano*, he thought to himself. He had no doubt the bartender had told Coppola about his visit to the bar the day before. He'd hit a nerve. Now he needed to figure out how to take advantage of the situation he'd provoked.

Vince was about to start his run when he noticed one of the Silverado's tires was flat. On closer inspection, it was clear it had been punctured by a sharp object. He also recognized that the puncture was in the tire's sidewall and nearly impossible to repair. The "Back off" message was now crystal clear.

Vince returned inside and found Ryan's truck keys. He quickly changed the flat and drove the truck to the Firestone store on Sam Rittenberg. The store had just opened, and he was lucky enough to get the tire replaced without waiting.

Back at the apartment, he found Ryan in the kitchen making coffee. "How was your run?" he asked.
~~~~

"Well, something came up, and I never got a chance to do it this morning."

"What do you mean?"

Vince explained the flattened tire and the text he'd received that morning. However, he didn't tell Ryan that the flattened tire was an apparent response to his visit to Callaghan's the day before.

"I took care of it, buddy," Vince said and explained he'd taken the truck to Firestone and had them replace the damaged tire. "It's pretty clear the text I got was from Coppola or his boss, Romano."

"We need to go to the police," Ryan said.

"We can certainly do that, but there's no way we can prove who did it."

"Coppola might have ordered it, but I still think Frank Romano must have been involved," Ryan said.

"Right," Vince agreed. "Whoever's behind it, I say we go down to the Lockwood station, tell that Officer Shaw about the tire, and see if he's heard anything about the Honda. We've heard nothing from Shaw, and it's been several days since we saw him."

Ryan agreed and said, "We should also check with Katy and see if the Mt. Pleasant police have learned anything new about Eddie Russo and what happened to her the other night. I'm also concerned it's been a few days since Katy identified that Alessio Messina fellow. I'm surprised Wadsworth hasn't brought Messina in for questioning. And you can bet that as soon as he does, Romano will know Katy identified Messina. That puts her in even more danger than she's already in."

"I'm afraid you're right," Vince said. "I'll go ahead and call her. I figure we can see Shaw later this morning and pick up Katy this afternoon."

"That works," Ryan said. He poured himself a cup of coffee and asked Vince how much the tire cost.

"Don't worry about that. I've got that covered. It's not your fault all this happened."

"At least let me pay for half," Ryan offered. "I know how tight things are for you."

"Thanks, but like I said, I got it covered," Vince said—realizing his visit to Callaghan's precipitated the whole thing.

<p style="text-align:center">~~~~</p>

They made it down to Lockwood around eleven that morning and waited about twenty minutes before Officer Shaw walked into the lobby.

"Mr. Kelly and Mr. Woods," he said, "what can I do for you?"

"Actually, a couple of things," Vince said. "It's been a while since we told you about the stolen Honda. Have you heard anything?"

"No, not a thing. But what information we have is in our system, and I'll let you know if anything turns up." Shaw glanced at his watch. "You said you have a couple of things. What else?"

Vince told Shaw about the punctured tire and the "Back off" text on his phone. "I don't think there's any doubt that text was sent from Michael Coppola, or maybe from his boss, Mr.

Romano. And you can bet that whoever sent that text was the one that destroyed the tire. We think it only goes to prove one of those groups was somehow behind my stolen Honda. What can you do about it?"

"Do you have any proof who actually did this to the tire?" Shaw asked.

"Well, no, but who else would do something like that and send a text telling me to back off?"

"Can you prove who sent the text?" Shaw questioned.

"No, but isn't it obvious?" Ryan said, frustration in his voice.

"We'll run the number from the text, but don't hold your breath. I can guarantee it was sent from a burner phone, which has been destroyed by now. I've passed on the information about the Honda and the note you found to the detectives working the Cornell Jackson homicide case. I'll let them know about the tire, but outside that, there's not much more I can do without solid evidence of who punctured your tire or sent that text."

Officer Shaw noted the phone number used to send the "Back off" text and said he'd run it and let them know if he came up with anything. He sounded less than enthusiastic.

Ryan and Vince were walking back to the truck when Ryan said, "That was pretty much what I expected. We can't prove anything. I'm thinking maybe it's time yow back off trying to get back the money for the Honda. I know it's a lot, but we're dealing with some dangerous people. Is it really worth it?"

"Yeah, but I can't see Coppola walking away as long as we pose a threat to him. We're pretty sure that Honda was used in the murder of Cornell Jackson, right? And Coppola and probably

Romano know both of us can identify the car and Eddie Russo. Plus, what happens to Katy when the cops arrest Romano's main guy, Messina? That makes us a liability to all of them, and they sure as hell know we're working with the cops. Don't forget Detective Wadsworth stopped by Callaghan's Bar and hassled Coppola."

"All that may be true," Ryan said, "but I still don't see a lot we can do about it."

"Maybe I can convince them it's to their advantage to give me back the six-grand Russo took from me," Vince said.

"Fat chance that'll happen," Ryan said.

~~~~

Vince glanced at his watch. "It's almost one. I told Katy we'd swing by to get her once we finished downtown."

As Ryan was leaving the station's parking lot, Vince's cell rang. He glanced at the number but didn't recognize it. He answered the call and listened for a good sixty seconds—broken only by a series of intermittent "Yes, sir's" and "No, sir's." The call was concluded with a simple, "Yes, sir. That will work fine, and thank you for the opportunity."

"Who was that?" Ryan asked.

"Remember that interdiction job I found on the internet?"

"Sure."

"Well, my friend, that was Chief Patrol Agent Perez from the U.S. Customs and Border Control. I've got a face-to-face interview with him tomorrow at two o'clock." Vince smiled.

"Really? That's great!"
~~~~

"Yeah, but I want to see how it goes before getting too excited."

"Don't be so modest. It's a perfect job for you. You'll nail it."

"I guess we'll see," Vince said, suppressing his excitement.

~~~~

They'd picked up Katy twenty minutes later, and Vince asked her if she wanted to get something to eat before seeing Detective Wadsworth.

"No, I've lost my appetite. Let's just go see him."

It was clear Katy was in a sour mood, and Vince knew it would take some time before she'd be able to shake it off. Vince decided to wait on telling Katy about his upcoming job interview until she had time to blow off some steam.

They arrived at the station and waited a few minutes before Detective Wadsworth appeared and walked them back to the conference room. The meeting was cordial, but it quickly became clear nothing new had been learned regarding the whereabouts of Eddie Russo. Vince brought the detective up to speed on Ryan's tire incident and threatening text he received. Wadsworth made a note of it but again indicated that it would fall under the jurisdiction of the Charleston police.

Ryan asked about Alessio Messina's arrest status since Katy had identified him as one of her assailants.

"I certainly appreciate your concern, and rest assured, nothing will be initiated related to Mr. Messina without first advising Ms. Pryor."
~~~~

"But it's been several days since Katy identified Messina," Vince pointed out. "Is there a reason nothing has been done yet?"

"Actually, there is," Wadsworth responded. "We know that Messina is Frank Romano's most trusted associate. Ms. Pryor identifying him as one of her assailants also exposes Mr. Romano and his entire organization to more scrutiny. We must be cautious about coordinating everything with the Charleston and North Charleston police departments, the city's task force on organized crime, and the respective district attorneys. Once we bring Messina in for questioning, there is a good chance he will be charged and arraigned for his assault on Ms. Pryor. Again, Ms. Pryor will be told what we intend to do before any effort is made to bring in Messina."

Vince and Ryan had a few more questions regarding when and how Messina would be brought in for questioning. Katy, however, had remained silent throughout the entire interview.

Ryan was driving Katy back to her apartment when Vince said, "Well, at least we know more about what's going to happen with Messina." Katy said nothing, and Vince asked if she was okay. Bad decision.

"Am I okay? Sure, Vince, I'm just peachy. Someone beat the hell out of me, and now some Mafia big wig knows about me. Yeah, Vince, I'm doing just fine. Take me home. I just want to go home."

Nobody said another word until Ryan dropped Katy off at her apartment.

"Let me know if you need anything," Vince called out. Without turning around, she raised her right hand and extended her middle finger in Vince's direction.

Ryan was pulling out of Katy's apartment complex when he said with a sardonic smile, "Well, that went well, don't you think?"

"Yeah, just dandy," Vince said. "I can't blame her for being mad. She had nothing to do with this whole thing, and now she's right smack-dab in the middle of it."

Back at the duplex, Vince mentioned that he'd never got a chance to take his run with everything that happened that morning. It was still relatively early, and he had time to get his five miles in before dinner.

About a mile or so into his run, Vince began to feel his endorphins kick in, and he settled into his average seven-minute mile pace. His daily jaunts had always been the best time for Vince to think. The hustle and bustle of everyday life melted away during his runs—allowing him to clear his mind and focus on the important matters at hand. The more he thought about the situation with Russo, the Honda, Coppola, the Jackson murder, and the attack on Katy, the more he felt responsible for the whole mess. And his two visits to Callaghan's hadn't really accomplished that much of anything. He also felt bad he didn't tell Ryan everything about those trips to Coppola's bar. The two of them had always been up front with each other. The more he mulled over everything, the more he realized that it was up to him to set things right. They'd certainly had little luck with the police. And there was something else. It was the creed he'd lived by for the past five years—Spiritus Invictus. *'Never quit. Never surrender. Never fail. Adapt to the situation. Gain and maintain the initiative.'*

Ryan was watching TV when Vince returned from his run. He got a bottle of water from the frig and joined Ryan in the living room. "Hey, buddy, I need to talk to you about a few things."

He felt like a jerk and let it all out. He finished by saying, "I've racked my brain trying to figure a way out of this. The only thing I do know is that walking away from a problem almost always leads to bigger problems down the road."

Ryan had listened to Vince but said nothing until he finished. "To be honest, I'm not surprised with what you did at that bar. You've never been someone who could turn his back on a bad situation. I've been thinking about the whole thing, too. The Honda would be evidence in the Jackson murder. That's got to be why it was stolen from in front of my place the other night. And like you said, whoever stole it has probably already destroyed it. The same thing goes with Eddie Russo. I'll bet whoever got rid of the Honda also made sure the Russo kid wouldn't be around Charleston anymore. I don't think there's any doubt that the cops know Coppola and Romano are behind the Jackson hit. Even if the car and the kid are gone, there's no way the police are going to stop the investigation until they find out who killed or ordered the killing of Cornell Jackson. So, where does that leave us?"

"Not good," Vince said, "but the more I thought about it, not as bad as you might think. I may be a pain in the ass for

Coppola and Romano, but if Russo and the Honda are gone, there's not much I can do to hurt either of them. That's not the case with Katy. Now that she can positively identify this Alessio Messina guy, the cops will bring him in for questioning, and like Wadsworth said, the DA will probably charge him with assault. I can't see anyway Messina will flip on his boss, but it still could cause a real shit storm for Romano and his organization."

"You're right," Ryan said, "and she shouldn't be alone at her apartment. Does she have any family in the area?"

"No, her dad died a few years ago, and her mom lives in California. Plus, the two of them don't get along all that well."

"Do you think she'd be willing to stay at my place?"

"I'll ask," Vince said, "but I know how hard-headed Katy can be. Even if we can persuade her to do it, don't forget both Coppola and Romano know where you live."

Vince called Katy and tried convincing her to come back to Ryan's apartment. Katy had cooled down by then and, while appreciating the offer, decided to stay put in her own apartment. She said she'd be extra careful, plus Detective Wadsworth told her as soon as Messina was brought into the station for questioning, the police would start monitoring her apartment. She promised to be careful but insisted she had a business to manage and a life to live and wasn't about to give those up.

CHAPTER 20

ON THE WAY back to Ryan's, Vince told him he intended to go to Callaghan's Bar to see what he could learn about Katy's situation and make one final attempt to find out where Eddie Russo might be hiding. Ryan wanted to come, but Vince nixed the idea. Knowing Vince had made up his mind, Ryan gave him the keys to the Silverado and said, "Listen, I know you're going to do this, but don't give me any of that Spiritus whatever stuff. Just please be careful and try not to provoke Coppola if he's there."

"I won't," Vince said. "I just want to give it one more shot. Just talk. That's all. I promise." He closed the door and left the apartment.

He arrived at Callaghan's and parked in the lot adjacent to the bar. He recognized the four cars parked in the lot—confirming Coppola, Sanborn, Big Mike, and the old bartender were there.

It was dark when Vince entered the bar, but his eyes almost immediately adjusted to the murky surroundings. The bartender sat alone in one of the barstools at the far end of the bar, and Big Mike could be seen standing sentinel behind the pool table in front of the door leading to Coppola's second-floor office. The only other occupants were an older couple seated in one of the booths against the wall—their glasses of amber-colored liquid resting in front of them.

Vince walked directly to the end of the bar, stopping in front of the bartender. This time there was no mock salute or congenial pretense.

"I want to talk to Mr. Coppola," Vince said, his eyes exhibiting a coldness the bartender had only witnessed in truly hard men.

The bartender rose, and before moving behind the bar to reach for his pistol, Vince grabbed the old man's shoulder and eased him back down onto the barstool. "Not this time," Vince said with an icy stare.

Witnessing what had just happened at the bar, Big Mike quickly opened the door behind him and called out, "Jimmy! I need you down here! Now!"

A few seconds later, Jimmy Sanborn appeared at the opened door—a concerned look on his face. "What's wrong?" he asked. But before the big man could answer, Sanborn saw Vince at the end of the bar holding his bartender's shoulder.

"The guy just got here. I didn't get a chance to …"

"Enough, Mike," Sanborn said and walked toward the bar. Remembering what the man did to Mike, he stopped about ten feet from Vince. He reached behind him and removed his .38 Special—the same gun Michael Coppola used fifteen years earlier to scare away the thugs who'd attacked Sanborn. Holding the gun by his side, he said, "I suggest you turn around and leave before someone gets hurt."

"I didn't come here for any trouble. But I'm not leaving until I talk to Coppola."

The couple in the booth got up and quickly left the bar when they saw the .38.

Sanborn raised his gun to his waist, its barrel trained on the center of Vince's chest. "Mr. Kelly, if you're asking about Eddie Russo, you're gonna get the same answer—haven't seen him, don't know where he is. Now, like I said, leave before …"

Sanborn was cut off by a voice from the back of the room. "Jimmy, check him to make sure he's not carrying." It was Michael Coppola.

Sanborn was surprised, to say the least, but he returned his gun to a leather holster attached to his belt at his lower back. He padded Vince down and said, "He's clean."

Coppola moved forward, stopping behind the far side of the pool table. Big Mike took up a position about ten feet to his right. Vince walked to the rear of the bar, stopping at the side of the pool table directly across from Coppola. Jimmy Sanborn, his gun held at his side, followed Vince until he was ten feet to the left of the pool table—flanking his boss.

"Mr. Kelly," Coppola began, "you are a persistent fellow. I understand you believe Eddie Russo took money from you, and you want it back. Whatever your dealings are with Eddie, they have nothing to do with me or my people. The truth is I don't care about the kid. I do, however, give a shit about you coming into my place and harassing my friends. You can deal with the Eddie kid yourself—just don't do it around here."

Vince stared at Coppola for a moment before saying, "We both know this is more than the six-grand your boy stole from me. And whatever that may be, my friends and I wanted no part of it. That changed when Russo attacked my wife, and as if that wasn't enough, you sent one of your goons to mess with my best friend's truck and sent me a threatening text."

"Hold it right there!" Coppola said. "I had nothing to do with what happened to your wife, and I know nothing about your friend's truck or any threatening text."

"Maybe not directly, but we both you and your people are involved," Vince said—trying hard to control his emotions. He gathered himself and went on, "Listen to me. We both know this has gone too far. You'll never see or hear from me again if you tell me where I can find Eddie Russo and promise to leave my wife and best friend out of this."

Michael Coppola was not used to being spoken to in such a blunt manner. Nor was he accustomed to being given what he considered an ultimatum—other than from Mr. Romano.

"First, I have no idea where Eddie Russo is, and even if I did, I wouldn't tell you. Second, I had nothing to do with your wife being attacked or your friend's truck. That is the truth. Now, you listen to me, Mr. Hard Ass. If I see or hear from you again, I'll be upset. And when I'm upset, people get hurt." He turned to Sanborn. "Jimmy, get him the hell out of here."

"You heard the man," Sanborn said. "Be smart and walk away."

Coppola couldn't gauge the look on Vince's face before he turned and left the bar. But whatever it was, he felt it may not be the last time he'd have to deal with Vince Kelly and was troubled by the implications of that.

CHAPTER 21

BACK IN THE Silverado, Vince locked the doors, started the truck, but didn't leave the lot. His head fell back against the headrest and his eyes closed. He'd hit hot spots for Coppola but accomplished little if nothing. Vince was less than proud of how he'd been acting over the last week or so. He was a Marine Raider, a member of one of the most elite fighting units in the whole of the United States military. And yet, he'd been hustled out of six grand by a twenty-some-year-old kid.

His first reaction was to respond like a Raider would: *Never quit. Never surrender. Never fail.* However, he had put both Katy— still one of the most important people in his life, and Ryan—his lifelong best friend, in jeopardy. Hell, Katy had been beaten badly, and Ryan's truck tire was ruined. He knew he would always be a Marine but getting used to his civilian life was more complex than he'd expected. Like Ryan said: "This is South Carolina, not Afghanistan." The rules have changed.

The loss of the $6,000 he paid for the Honda and the $400 for Ryan's tire still stung, but it wasn't worth what he'd done to his friends. Plus, he had a good feeling about the interdiction job and the upcoming interview with Chief Patrol Officer Perez and didn't want to do anything to mess it up. He would talk to Katy and Ryan Tuesday evening and tell them that he no longer intended to pursue Eddie Russo or his dealings with Michael Coppola.

~~~~

Tuesday morning passed uneventfully. Ryan left early to attend a computer class required to satisfy the State's Continuing Education Units and maintain his teaching certification. Katy's face still bore the remnants of her attack, but her stitches had been removed, and she was now able to spend more time in her real estate office catching up with clients and dealing with the mounting paperwork. Vince enjoyed his morning run and spent an hour doing some further internet research on the job description and requirements for his upcoming interview. He passed the balance of the morning doing odds and ends needed to get ready to move into his new apartment.

Vince spent a half-hour fussing over what to wear for his job interview. He finally finished dressing and took an Uber to the U.S. Customs and Border Protection offices on East Bay Street. At two o'clock sharp, Vince was met by Chief Patrol Officer James Perez and walked back to a conference room. Two other agents were in the room, which Perez introduced.
~~~~

There were a few minutes of small talk before Perez began the formal interview by explaining what the position entailed. Vince had a few questions, and the other two agents added their thoughts.

Twenty minutes later, Perez got down to business. "Mr. Kelly, we are impressed with your career in the Marines. We've been in contact with your unit commander, Captain Charles Rice. Captain Rice's opinion of your performance while under his command could not have been more positive."

There was a short lull in the conversation during which Perez looked at the two other agents in the room. Both nodded, and he rose and asked Vince if he would please take a seat outside the conference room for a few moments. He walked Vince outside and returned to the room, shutting the door behind him. Perez reappeared five minutes later and told Vince to join them back in the conference room.

"Vince, we've done our homework and have seen what we need to see. We all agree you'd make a good addition to our team here in Charleston. The entry-level compensation for the position will be at level GS-9, Step 1 or approximately $66,000, and of course, that will be augmented with the health and other standard government benefit packages." It was Perez's turn to smile. "How does that sound, Vince?"

Vince was a bit shocked by the offer. He'd assumed that this meeting would be one in a series of interviews before any job would or would not be offered. He quickly regained his composure and answered with a simple, "That sounds great, sir."

"Good," Perez said, stood, and extended his hand. "Welcome aboard!" Vince exchanged handshakes and congratulations from the other two agents. "Come with me, and I'll introduce you to Jim Kagan. He'll get you started on the paperwork."

"Thank you, sir," Vince said. "When do you expect I'll start?"

Perez grinned. "You know how the government works. I figure in about two weeks, but I'll let you know the specific date within the next few days." Perez shook Vince's hand again and said, "Oh, and by the way, Semper Fi."

The surprise on Vince's face was evident. "You're a Marine, sir?"

"Once a Marine, always a Marine," Perez answered. "Left the Corps as a Major 16 years ago. Spent several tours in Afghanistan. So, I'm sure we'll have some stories to share." He turned to Jim Kagan. "Jim, Mr. Kelly is all yours."

~~~~

Vince spent another hour dealing with the required government forms and paperwork before leaving the office, genuinely excited! He couldn't wait to tell his mom, Ryan, and Katy.

He called his mom at the library as soon as he left to give her the good news. Shelly was elated and surprised Vince with some good news of her own. "You've met my good friend, Irene Sheridan, the lady who works with me at the library?"
~~~~

"Sure," Vince laughed. "If you're not home, you're either at work or out somewhere with her."

"I guess you're right about that. Irene and I made a decision, and it's not open for discussion. Her daughter is spending a college semester in Europe this summer. Her car is just sitting in the garage, and Irene insists you use it until you start your new job and can buy one. Now don't argue. I've already got insurance on the car for you. Irene said you can return it when you start work and get one for yourself."

"No way, Mom!" Vince insisted. "I can get by using Ryan's truck and Katy's car."

"Sorry, son, it's a done deal. Irene really wants to do this."

Vince had to admit that it would be nice not to continue to ask to use Ryan's truck and Katy's car. Plus, he knew his mom was just as hard-headed as he was.

"Are you sure about this, Mom?"

"Of course, I am. The only catch is that you have to bring Ryan and Katy over for lunch on Sunday. Irene is driving the car over in the morning, and I'll drive her back. You can get it then."

"All right, Mom. You two didn't have to do this, but thanks. I promise I'll make it up to both of you."

"Oh, stop it," Shelly said. "This is what mothers do. Now, I'll see you on Sunday."

"Thanks again, Mom. See you Sunday."

~~~~
~~~~

Vince got a hold of Ryan and Katy and told them he had a few things he needed to share with them but wouldn't say what they were until they got together that evening. They agreed to meet at P.F. Chang's, located in Mt. Pleasant directly across from Katy's apartment complex.

Ryan and Vince arrived at Chang's at 7:00 that evening, with Katy showing up ten minutes later. Sitting at the bar, Vince ordered three beers and said, "I want to apologize to both of you for how I've acted lately." He explained how selfish he'd been and how bad he felt that his actions had involved both of them because of the way he'd dealt with Russo, Coppola, and Romano. He promised he was finished with the whole thing. He accepted the fact that he was out the $6,000, but he'd get by. It was clear that both Ryan and Katy were relieved to hear the news.

"That's certainly good news," Katy said, "Now, you said you had a few things to tell us. What else?"

Vince broke the news about his new job. Ryan and Katy could not have been happier for him. They had another round, and Vince insisted on buying dinner for everyone. It was a great evening with not another word spoken of Eddie Russo, Michael Coppola, or Frank Romano.

Wednesday passed without incident. Ryan attended his computer class, and Katy caught up with her real estate business. Without much to do, Vince extended his run, spent a few hours cleaning Ryan's duplex, and ordered a few more things his mother insisted he'd need for the apartment.

Things changed Thursday morning when Katy received a call from Detective Wadsworth. The necessary coordination between jurisdictions had been established, allowing Wadsworth and his officers to bring in Alessio Messina.

"Before I say anything else, it is imperative that everything I tell you remains confidential once we have Mr. Messina in custody. The task force has been monitoring Alessio Messina for some time and knows he leaves his home every Friday at around two o'clock and drives to Mr. Romano's Import business located in the North Charleston's Westview Industrial Park off of 526. We're planning on apprehending him as he is leaving his apartment. By arresting and charging him later Friday afternoon, he won't be arraigned in court until Monday morning, which will allow us to hold him in jail over the weekend.

"Based on the extent of the assault, Mr. Messina would normally only be charged with second-degree assault and battery, which is a misdemeanor in South Carolina. Even with his prior convictions, he's likely to get only a relatively minimal jail time and a fine of a few thousand dollars. Our people are getting pressure from the task force on organized crime to charge Messina. We have also obtained a search warrant for Mr. Messina's apartment which will be exercised as soon as we have him in custody."

"What am I supposed to do?" asked Katy.

"We will need you to formally identify Messina in a lineup on Saturday. You will be behind a one-way mirror, so he will not be able to see you. In the meantime, I would just recommend you make sure you secure your apartment doors and be aware of your surroundings. If you go out, make sure someone knows where you're going, and it would be a good idea to go with another person, if possible. Call the station if you notice anything out of the ordinary. Starting Friday afternoon, I've made arrangements for a team in each shift to make periodic drive-by checks of your apartment."

"But I sell real estate. I'm meeting with people and showing properties all the time."

"I understand, Ms. Pryor. All I'm saying is to take some extra precautions. Again, I don't think you have much to worry about for the time being. I'll be checking in with you every day or two, and please let me know if you have any questions or concerns."

When Katy disconnected the call, she felt like throwing her phone against the wall. *Jesus Christ*, she thought, *questions or concerns?* She moped around her apartment for a while before realizing she should let Vince and Ryan know what was in the works for tomorrow afternoon.

She called Vince.

"Hey, Katy. How are you doing?"

"Dandy, Vince. Just dandy." She proceeded to pass on the information she'd just received from Detective Wadsworth. It was clear she was beyond pissed. "What the hell am I supposed to do now. I've got clients I need to take care of. Wadsworth tells me to be aware of my surroundings, and it would be a good idea to take someone with me if I go out. I've got a damn real estate business to run. I can't do that."

The line was quiet, but Vince could hear Katy's exaggerated breathing. "I'm sorry, Katy. Let me think. This whole thing sucks, but there's no way you should be staying at your apartment by yourself. You should stay with Ryan and me at his place."

"I'm not doing that. End of discussion."

"Okay, then let me stay at your place," Vince said.

"That's not going to happen," Katy answered emphatically. "Listen, I've got to meet some new clients at the office. The detective said nothing was going to happen until tomorrow. I'm showing the couple property in West Ashley at four o'clock this afternoon. I'll stop by Ryan's when I'm finished showing it, and we'll talk more then."

~~~~

The pleasure Vince had experienced the last few days was now replaced with a palpable sense of regret for his part in putting Katy in the dangerous position. While the threat from Coppola seemed to have been lessened, that was now being replaced by a more foreboding risk—Romano's crime organization.

Ryan returned from his class at three that afternoon, and Vince recounted the conversation he'd had with Katy that morning.

Ryan listened carefully but said nothing until his friend was finished. He remained silent for a moment before saying, "I've been thinking about what Katy should do ever since we learned she'd identified the Messina guy. She definitely should not be staying at her apartment."

"I tried that already," Vince said, "but she said she's staying put. She's one stubborn lady."
~~~~

"Something doesn't make sense," Ryan said. "You said that without evidence that the cash and necklace were taken during Katy's assault, the best the DA could hope for is a misdemeanor which sounds like nothing more than a slap on the wrist. The thing is, it's going to be Katy's word against Messina's. Remember when Detective Wadsworth and that tech checked her apartment for fingerprints. Messina's prints were never found there, and his prints sure as hell would have been in the system. Plus, you can bet Messina will be lawyered up a half-hour after he gets to the station tomorrow. And you know Romano will have a solid alibi for Messina as soon as he knows the charges."

"Exactly," Vince agreed, "and how will Katy prove she had the cash in her wallet—much less that my grandma's necklace was taken?"

"You said Wadsworth's people have a search warrant for Messina's apartment," Ryan said. "It's a long shot, but maybe they'll find something there. I can see how the cops would love to get to Romano by nailing Messina. I'm no lawyer, but the cops better have a hell of a lot more than just Katy's ID of Messina."

"You're right," Vince agreed, "and to be perfectly honest, I hope the whole thing blows up in their face, and the Messina dude walks. As long as Katy poses no threat the Romano, maybe he's got no reason to worry about her."

Katy showed up at Ryan's about 5:30 that evening. They ordered pizza and spent an hour rehashing what Vince and Ryan had already discussed.

There was a somewhat lengthy pause in the conversation before Vince asked what would happen if Katy refused to identify Messina in a lineup. Would the police just drop the whole case? Would that be enough for Romano to back off?

"I have no idea," Katy said. "I suppose I could refuse to do it, but it would irk the hell out of me knowing that these assholes got away with what they did to me."

It was clear nothing more would be accomplished that night, and Katy left with the understanding Vince and Ryan would meet her at her apartment at two o'clock Friday afternoon and wait for a call from Detective Wadsworth confirming Alessio Messina was in custody.

CHAPTER 22

VINCE DROPPED RYAN off at 8:30 Friday morning for his computer class and killed the rest of his morning by adding a few miles to his regular run and searching the web for different types of cars or trucks he could afford once he started his new job.

Vince picked up Ryan at one o'clock, and they made it out to Katy's a half-hour later. She wasn't there when they arrived, and the boys waited until almost two o'clock before she finally showed up.

Katy let them in, and Vince asked how she was holding up.

"I'm good," she replied. "It's been a crazy busy morning at work which was actually a good thing. It kept my mind off what's going to happen today. I figured it would be a while before we hear from the detective, so I bought some snacks and soft drinks."

"I don't know about you guys," Ryan jumped right in, "but all I've had today is a cup of coffee and a bagel. I say we order something."

"I can go out, or we can just order a pizza," Vince offered.

"Please, no more pizza," Ryan pleaded. "I feel like I've had it every other night."

"I agree," Katy said. "I'll tell you what I haven't had in ages—McDonald's. I could use a big order of Chicken McNuggets and fries. And throw in a medium chocolate milkshake."

"I'm in," Vince said. "A double cheeseburger and fries sound good to me. How about you, Ryan?"

"A Big Mac and fries and maybe a chocolate cookie for good measure. Hell, we got beer. I'd say we've covered all the major food groups."

Vince drove Ryan's truck to the Golden Arches and returned twenty minutes later with the food—which was devoured in short order. Katy hammered away on her computer for the next few hours, and the boys settled in behind the TV, watching the movie *Field of Dreams* and arguing who had seen it more times.

Around five o'clock, Detective Wadsworth called, informing Katy the arrest of Alessio Messina went off without a hitch, and he was currently in custody. As expected, one of Romano's lawyers named Evan Guthrie, showed up when Messina was being processed at the station. There was little Guthrie could do other than advise Messina not to answer any questions. Before hanging up, Wadsworth promised to call back when the forensic team concluded the search of Messina's apartment.

Katy passed on the information, and for the next several hours, Katy and the boys took in some movies on Netflix and watched and listened to the Fourth of July fireworks.

Detective Wadsworth called at 9:00 that evening to update Katy on what had transpired since his last call.

"Thanks for calling back, detective. Vince Kelly and Ryan Woods are here with me. I'm putting your call on speaker so they can hear."

"That's fine, Ms. Pryor. I would only insist that what we discuss remains confidential. I understand your friends are, to a degree, involved in this. However, the recent developments in the case have been significant. These developments mustn't become public in any form. Do I make myself clear?"

"I understand," Katy replied. Both Vince and Ryan also agreed.

"Good," Wadsworth said. "First of all, our district attorney has currently charged Mr. Messina with assault and battery. As I already explained, this charge is only a misdemeanor but can carry one year in prison and a fine of up to $2,500. Even with Mr. Messina's previous convictions in Charleston and Chicago, it's doubtful he would serve anywhere near the maximum if convicted."

Before Wadsworth could continue, Vince said, "This is Vince Kelly, detective. You mentioned a series of recent developments. What are they?"

"I was just getting to that. We've retrieved copies of the security tapes from the Thickett Apartments the night Ms. Pryor was attacked. The recordings revealed two men approaching Katy's apartment at 9:20 that night. Like many older security systems, the tape was black and white and grainy. The men's faces could not be identified; however, one individual wore jeans and a windbreaker. The second man, much larger than his partner, wore a sports jacket and loose-pleated slacks.

"The two men approached apartment #113 and knocked," Wadsworth continued. "A moment later, the door opened. There was a brief conversation, and the video showed the man wearing the windbreaker breaking down the door and entering the apartment. The larger man followed him in. One minute and thirteen seconds later, both men exited the apartment and left the premises."

It was Vince who again interrupted. "But you said the men's faces couldn't be identified."

"Correct," Wadsworth calmly replied. "The low quality of the security tape didn't allow for positive identification of either man, but our computer techs have good enhancement software that may be able to sharpen the images. The last footage showed them exiting the entrance to the apartment complex. Our people obtained security videos from several businesses located directly across I-17 in the Towne Centre Shopping Mall. The video from the Verizon store was of much higher quality than the one given to us by the apartment complex. It showed that at approximately 9:16, a late model Dodge Charger had arrived and parked in the Verizon lot, and two men matching the same general appearance in the apartment's tapes exited the vehicle. Nine minutes later, at 9:25, the Verizon video showed the same two men returning to the store's parking lot, getting into the Charger, and leaving the lot. Even though the Verizon tape could not identify the men's faces, it did show a South Carolina license plate of LMC-421. That particular plate was issued to an Alessio Messina."

Wadsworth explained that the Charger returned about thirty-five minutes later. Ten minutes after that, the car left the lot and turned right onto Highway 17.

"Hold on," Vince said, "I'm not exactly sure, but I think that's about the same time we left Katy's apartment to take her to Doctor's Care."

"Interesting," Wadsworth said, "but that doesn't prove they were following you."

It was Katy who now questioned the detective. "Is all this enough to prove they were the men that attacked me?"

"Perhaps not, but there's more evidence our people uncovered. To our surprise, one of the items recovered from Messina's apartment was the necklace given to you the day of your wedding. It matches the pictures you gave us. As you know, there are a few decent-sized emeralds inlaid in it. These stones were large enough to allow our techs to dust for fingerprints. The prints were scanned back at the lab, and four positive hits were discovered. Yours was obviously one. The others included Mr. Eddie Russo's and 16-point partials for Mr. Alessio Messina and a Mr. Samuel Amato."

"Who's Samuel Amato?" Vince asked. "I never heard anyone talk about that guy."

"Sammy Amato works for Frank Romano," Wadsworth replied. "He is what is termed the Organization's muscle. Amato has been linked to at least two murders in Charleston, but the police lacked enough evidence to charge him in both cases. We are making plans to bring him in for questioning. The fact that the fingerprints of Russo, Messina, and Amato are present on the stolen necklace will allow our DA to add larceny to the assault charge. We are having the necklace appraised, but there's no doubt its value will exceed $2,000. That will change the larceny charge to grand larceny, making it a felony."

"So, what happens next?" Katy asked.

"I would like you to come down to the station at one o'clock tomorrow. We are arranging a lineup during which you can confirm the identity of Mr. Messina as one of the individuals that was present at the time of your assault. That will add another critical element of evidence to the case. Mr. Messina will be arraigned at nine Monday morning. At that time, he will be formally charged and allowed to plead guilty or not guilty. He will definitely plead not guilty, and the subject of bail will be discussed. It is the purview of the judge to set the bail amount. We don't know what that amount might be. But we do know that whatever the amount, bail will be arranged, and Mr. Messina should be free to leave custody later that morning."

"What do I do?" Katy asked. "Just show up at the police station a little before one tomorrow."

"Actually, no," Wadsworth replied. "You'll be picked up by two of our officers in an unmarked squad car. They will escort you into the station through a rear entrance. I will be with you in the lineup room. The lineup itself should only take a few minutes. The officers will then return you to your apartment. If you have any questions, please call me at the station. I should be there by eight tomorrow morning."

~~~~

Katy thanked the detective and disconnected the call.

"How do you feel about all this?" Ryan asked.

"To be honest, I feel like a pawn in a chess game that's about to be sacrificed. I get the feeling Romano's lawyer—I forget his name."

"Guthrie," Vince answered.

"Yeah, Guthrie," Katy said. "I get the feeling he'll figure out a way to discount all of the evidence Wadsworth just told us or come up with some technicality to dismiss the whole thing."

"I don't think anyone knows what will happen," Vince offered. "But I bet the cops and DA's figure this is their best shot to get at Romano's organization, and they could care less how it affects you."

"That's a pleasant thought," Katy said. "It's been a long day. I just want to go to sleep."

"Katy," Ryan said, "It's already ten o'clock. Is it okay if we hang around and spend the night?"

"That's fine," she said.

"Ryan, you can take the second bedroom," Vince said, "and I'll sleep on the couch." Vince managed a smile. "It won't be the first time. Right, Katy?"
~~~~

Even with everything that had happened, Katy managed to return the smile. "Yeah, I guess you should be used to that."

The three of them were settled in for the night by eleven o'clock.

Vince was sleeping soundly until around four in the morning when something woke him. He sat up on the couch and saw Katy getting a glass of water in the kitchen.

"Katy?" Vince questioned.

"I'm sorry, Vince. Can't sleep very well. I guess my brain's working overtime. You want a glass of water?"

"Sure."

Katy poured another glass and gave it to Vince—who was by now awake. "Thanks."

Both were quiet for a time until Katy said, "I'm scared."

"I know, but just remember both Ryan and I are here for you no matter what."

"I appreciate that," she said. "I'm sorry I woke you up. Go back to sleep. I'll see you in the morning." She bent down and gave Vince a gentle kiss on his forehead, went back to her bedroom, and closed the door behind her.

~~~~

Katy and the boys were up in the kitchen having coffee when there was a knock on the door. Vince told Katy to stay put. He unlocked the door and released the deadbolt before opening the door while leaving the security chain intact.
~~~~

There were two uniformed police officers outside the apartment. "Good morning, sir. I'm Officer White, and this is my partner Officer Reilly. Detective Wadsworth assigned us to periodically check in on Ms. Pryor. Is she home?"

Katy heard the conversation and joined Vince. "I'm Katy Pryor."

"Good morning, Ms. Pryor." Officer White reintroduced his partner and himself and said, "We'll be driving by your apartment several times every hour during our shift, as will other officers during their shifts. Please let us know if you need us for any reason. You can call 911, and they'll get us the message. Have a nice day, ma'am."

The officers left, and Vince relocked the door.

"That's good to know," Vince said. "If it's okay with you, Ryan and I will hang around until you leave for that lineup."

"That's fine, but I want you guys to go back to Ryan's. You got things to do. You heard what the officer said. I love you guys, but I need my privacy."

Vince knew better than to argue with Katy once her mind was set on something.

"Wait a second. I almost forgot," Vince said, "You remember my mom's good friend and coworker, Irene Sheridan."

"Sure. Nice lady."

"Anyway, apparently her daughter, Lily, is in Europe this summer, and her car is just sitting in the garage. Mrs. Sheridan wants me to use it until I start my job and buy one. Mom's already got insurance on the car for me. She said I can pay her back after I start work."

"That's amazingly nice of both of them!"

"I tried to talk my mom out of it, but you can imagine how that went. The only thing she made me promise is that you and Ryan have to stop by her house tomorrow for lunch. Does that work for you two?"

"Cool," Ryan said, and Katy enthusiastically agreed.

The three of them had a quiet morning until about 12:30 when two more officers arrived in an unmarked police car, showed their IDs, and said they were there to take Katy to the police station. She promised to call Vince as soon as she finished the lineup and left with the officers. The boys locked the apartment up tight before driving back to Ryan's.

CHAPTER 23

WHEN THE SQUAD car arrived at the Mt. Pleasant police station, Detective Wadsworth was waiting by one of the rear doors and walked Katy to the room where she would view the men assembled for the lineup.

There were three other individuals in the room—two men and one woman. One of the men was an officer who would operate the video equipment used to record the process.

The detective first introduced Katy to the woman. "This is Elizabeth Wells, Katy. Ms. Wells is our city's district attorney." Katy and Wells shook hands. Wadsworth introduced the man as Mr. Evan Guthrie, Alessio Messina's attorney. Katy simply nodded.

District Attorney Wells began explaining what would happen during the lineup process. "I realize this is the first time you've done something like this, and it's perfectly natural to be nervous. It will help if you try to relax and take your time. The process shouldn't last long, but there's absolutely no rush. This is termed a simultaneous lineup, which means you will be viewing the suspect in a group with other men called fillers. Most of these fillers will have similar features to the suspect—things like age, height and build, hair length, etc. You will also be viewing these men through a one-way mirror, so no one on the other side will be able to see you. The men will be told to turn to their sides so you can also see their profiles. Each man will have a number hanging around their neck. If you recognize the suspect, identify him only by the number he is wearing. Again, try to relax and take your time. If you identify one of the men in the lineup, you will need to sign a statement confirming the identification and the degree of your certainty. Any questions?"

"No, not really," Katy answered.

"Oh," Wells said, "I almost forgot. If you would like one or more of the men to repeat a short phrase, ask Detective Wadsworth."

"Got it," Katy replied.

"Good," DA Wells said and nodded at Detective Wadsworth to begin the process. The detective picked up the wall phone, punched in a number, and gave the go-ahead to bring in the participants.

A moment later, six men entered the room in the reverse order of the number they wore. Alessio Messina was the second from the end, wearing the number 5 around his neck.

The moment he appeared, Katy whispered to Wadsworth, "I see him."

Wadsworth quickly told her to say nothing more until the men showed their profiles. Once the six men were settled in the lineup, they were told to turn to their right showing their left profile, and then to the left, exposing their right. DA Wells and Evan Guthrie were almost wholly focused on Katy's demeanor as she watched the men.

About a minute into the process, Wadsworth asked Katy if she wanted the men to repeat a phrase. "You don't have to, but you can if you think it would help."

She thought a while and told Wadsworth to have each man repeat the phrase, "Is Vince Kelly here?"

Wadsworth passed on the request, and each man repeated the phrase.

"Anything else?" DA Wells asked.

"No. If that's all I need to do, I can tell you who he is."

"Go ahead," Wells said, "but only use his number rather than his name."

"Number 5 is the man that was at my door the night I was attacked. I am absolutely positive of that."

Attorney Guthrie hadn't said a word throughout the entire process and quietly left the viewing room.

As soon as Guthrie left the room, Elizabeth Wells put her hand on Katy's shoulder and said, "You did an excellent job, Ms. Pryor. Just relax for a few minutes while the area is cleared, and then we can have you sign those documents."

Wadsworth picked up the phone and gave instructions that the men could be released, and Messina returned to this cell.

Detective Wadsworth thanked Katy for her help and said the officers who had picked her up earlier would return her to her apartment as soon as the documents were completed.

Forty-five minutes later, the officers arrived at Katy's apartment. Once confirming it was secure, they let her in.

It was only 2:30 that afternoon, and after updating the boys on how the lineup went, she left to put in a few hours at her office.

~~~~

"So, what you're saying is the bitch not only identified Alessio but also asked him to say something about Vince Kelly," Frank Romano said, his anger apparent.

"That's exactly what I just said," Guthrie calmly replied. "It was clear she identified Messina the moment he entered the lineup. As far as I know, there's no direct evidence Messina even assaulted the woman. She only had a fraction of a second to see his face. Plus, it was nighttime. The only charge is an assault which is a misdemeanor. That's a relatively minor offense in South Carolina. To tell you the truth, the Russo kid presents a bigger problem, but again, his involvement is only circumstantial at best."

"Forget about Russo. How do we make this go away?"

"The arraignment is at nine Monday morning. We'll plead not guilty, and the judge will set bail. I should have Messina out on bail by noon. To be honest, if this is all they've got, I can't see the DA even pursuing the case. I think this is being done to simply hassle you and the Organization."
~~~~

"Well, they're doing a good job of pissing me off," Romano said and stood. "Like I said, do what you need to do to make this disappear."

~~~~

Katy returned to her place at seven. A few minutes later, she got a call from Vince, ensuring she was okay and confirming he would meet her at his mom's house around 12:30 pm tomorrow for lunch.

Around eight that evening, two Mt. Pleasant uniformed officers showed up at Katy's door. They showed their identification and introduced themselves. They explained they would be periodically checking her apartment during their shifts.

"We'll be close by, Ms. Pryor, so call 911, and they'll contact us if you need anything. Also, if you leave your apartment, please let us know where you're going."

Katy thanked the policemen, locked her door, and spent a quiet evening, falling asleep at ten o'clock.

~~~~

Ryan and Vince left at noon the following day for their lunch with Vince's mom. When Ryan pulled up in front of Shelly's house 35 minutes later, he started to chuckle. A not-so-new, lime green Volkswagen was sitting in the driveway with a dented rear fender and a few other dings.

Ryan said with a smile, "I'd better park in the street. I don't want to squoosh that Bug in the driveway."

"Well, at least it's got four wheels," Vince finally said, "and you should be happy I won't be hitting you up to use your truck."

Ryan went ahead and pulled in next to the Volkswagen, and they got out of the Silverado and began checking it out. Besides a minor dent in the fender, the car seemed to be in decent shape. It was clear both the interior and exterior had been thoroughly cleaned.

"Actually," Ryan said, "it's not bad, as long as you can fit in it."

The boys spent a few more minutes examining the VW until Katy pulled up and parked on the street. She got out of her car and started to laugh. "Nice wheels, Vincent. A real chick-magnet you got there."

Vince turned to Ryan. "Chick-magnet? Nobody says chick magnet anymore. That went out decades ago."

Ryan smiled and said, "Well, buddy, it looks like your little Bug is bringing *chick-magnet* back in style."

Katy had just started walking towards the house when Shelly appeared at the front door. She smiled and called out, "Katy, come here and give me a hug!" Katy and Vince had their ups and downs, but Katy had always been close to Shelly— perhaps due to the ongoing troubles with her own mother.

"I've missed you, sweetie," Shelly said. They hugged, and Shelly whispered, "Vince told me about all the terrible things you're going through. I'm so sorry, but no more talk of that. Come inside. We need to catch up on things."

"Hey, how about number two son," Ryan called out. "Did you forget about me?"

"Come over here, number two," she said and gave Ryan a hug.

"How about number one son?" Vince asked as he put his arm around his mom. "Oh, and before I forget, I need Irene's phone number. I want to call her and thank her for letting me use her daughter's Volkswagen. It'll be great."

Shelly smiled and said, "Oh, stop it. It's a tiny little green car, but that's nice of you to say. Now, all of you come inside. I've got some munchies before we have lunch."

Once inside, Shelly asked, "Now, what can I get everyone to drink? Boys, I've got your beer, and Katy, I also have some white wine."

"Ryan and I'll have beer, Mom," Vince said. "How about you, Katy?"

She turned to Shelly. "Do you have iced tea or a soft drink? I'm showing some houses later this afternoon."

"How about iced tea?" Shelly offered.

"Iced tea would be great," Katy answered and remembered she'd forgotten to call 911, so the officers on duty knew where she'd was. She excused herself and made the call, giving them Shelly's address and that she would be with clients from about 4:00 until around 7:00 that evening and then back to her apartment.

Katy returned to the living room, where everyone chatted about a myriad of things for the next few hours, including Vince's new job, Ryan's teaching, and Katy's real estate business.

Finally, Vince checked his watch and noticed it was already past two o'clock. "Hey, Mom, we should probably eat pretty soon. Remember Katy has to be at her office this afternoon."

"Oh, dear, the time got away from me. Come on in the kitchen. I have sandwiches, potato salad, and all the fixings."

Everyone served themselves and returned to the living room, where Shelly had brought out folding tables to eat off of. They ate and talked for the next forty-five minutes. Shelly brought everyone up to date on her noisy neighbors and the latest gossip from the library.

Around 3:00 o'clock, Katy stood and said, "Shelly, it's so good to see you, but I better get to my office. I've got to finish putting some information together for my clients."

"Of course, dear. Now don't be a stranger. I miss our lunches."

"I miss them, too," Katy quickly replied, "I promise I'll call."

Shelly walked Katy to the door, and after another hug and more thank yous, Katy left for her office. Vince and Ryan spent another hour or so at the house.

Before they left, Ryan patted Vince's back and said in an overly dramatic voice, "I'd better follow you back to my place just in case your Bug dies on the way."

"Good idea," Vince said with a grin.

Vince and Ryan each backed out of the driveway and made their way back to West Ashley, where they spent a quiet evening watching TV.

CHAPTER 24

ELIZABETH WELLS, THE city's district attorney, and Alessio Messina and his defense attorney, Evan Guthrie, were seated at their respective tables when Judge Judith Walker entered the Mt. Pleasant municipal courtroom. She took a seat at the bench, nodded at the two attorneys, and lightly tapped her gavel. Her attention shifted to her court bailiff. "Let's get started. What do we have today?"

The bailiff read off the case number and charges against Alessio. Guthrie had only received a copy of the modified indictment late Saturday and had been surprised the charge against his client was now a Class D felony because of the addition of grand larceny to the original assault.

The judge read Alessio his constitutional rights and asked Guthrie how his client pleads?

"Not guilty, your Honor, and Mr. Messina requests his right to a speedy trial."

"All right," the judge said and referred to her court calendar. "My first available court date is Monday, September 12th." She asked both Wells and Guthrie if that was acceptable. They both responded in the affirmative. "Good, let's move on to the subject of bail. Ms. Wells, what are the prosecution's recommendations?"

"Yes, your Honor," Wells replied, "Mr. Messina has two prior convictions and has been known to associate with certain criminal elements in Charleston. Based on that, the severity of the crime, and our belief Mr. Messina poses a flight risk, we would recommend bail be set at two hundred thousand dollars."

The judge shifted her attention to Guthrie. "Your response, Mr. Guthrie?"

"Your Honor, the two prior convictions Ms. Wells referred to were only misdemeanors. Mr. Messina is gainfully employed, has lived in Charleston for two years, owns a home, and presents no flight risk. We would request Mr. Messina be released on his own recognizance without a bail requirement."

Judge Walker thought for a moment. She was well aware of Messina's relationship with Frank Romano and his organization. "Thank you both. Bail will be set at seventy-five thousand dollars." Walker asked her bailiff to read the following case on the docket.

Court officers returned Messina to custody until bail was arranged. Guthrie caught up with Wells as she was leaving the courtroom. "What's this about adding grand larceny to the indictment? The original charge was only a misdemeanor."

"Come on, Evan. You're an attorney. You know what grand larceny means. We just happened to find new evidence, including the fact that your client was involved in the theft of some rather expensive jewelry during his assault on Ms. Pryor."

"What evidence?"

Not wanting to say anything about the prints found on the necklace, Wells simply said, "Let's just wait for discovery. That should clear up any questions you might have." Wells smiled. "Have a nice day, Evan."

Guthrie called Frank Romano to advise him of the situation. Romano wasn't happy and ordered both Alessio and him to come directly to his office at the industrial park as soon as possible. It took a few hours for Guthrie to arrange bail and have Alessio processed out of the correctional center before leaving for Romano's office.

~~~~

Romano was clearly pissed when Evan and Alessio stepped into his office. "What the hell is going on, Guthrie? You told me you could make this go away. Now you say we've got a felony on our hands."

There was a bit of embarrassment in Guthrie's voice when he answered, "From what the district attorney said, they have new evidence that Alessio was involved in a theft of some jewelry when the Russo kid busted down the Pryor girl's apartment door."
~~~~

Romano's eyes were now directly on Alessio. "Stolen jewelry? What's this all about? Did you take anything from that woman?"

"No, boss. The kid must have taken a necklace while we were at her apartment."

"Where's the necklace now?" Romano asked.

"Apparently, the DA has it."

"How did that happen?"

Not wanting to talk about the killing of Eddie Russo in front of Guthrie, Alessio said, "The kid gave me the necklace, and I had it at my place. I was going to show it to my fence to see if it was worth anything. The cops had a search warrant for my place and must have found it there."

"Jesus Christ, Alessio," Frank said before asking Guthrie what he would do about the case now.

"We'll know more about what they've got during discovery," Guthrie answered. "From what the DA said, they may have more evidence linking Alessio to the necklace and the assault. If that's the case, the Pryor woman's testimony now becomes our biggest problem."

"Okay," Romano said, "Guthrie, you can get the hell out of here and keep me informed of where we are on this. Alessio, you stay."

As soon as Guthrie was gone, Romano said, "Christ, Alessio, I thought you were smarter than that. Now my ass is on the line with our friends in Chicago." He was quiet for a moment before continuing, "Can you still contact the gray-haired man we used to get rid of Cornell Jackson?"

"Yeah, he gave me the number to one of his burners encase we need him again."

"Good, he owes us one for fucking up the Jackson job. Get ahold of him and tell him I expect him in my office at 9:00 tomorrow morning. And tell him to drive. I don't need any paper trails on this."

Alessio left Romano's office and did as he was told. The gray-haired man knew Romano could damage his professional reputation within the criminal underground and realized he had little choice but to agree.

CHAPTER 25

ROMANO WAS ALONE when he met the gray-haired man the following morning. He ushered the man into his office, pointed to the chair in front of his desk, and coldly ordered, "Sit!" He paused a moment while the man did as he was told. "Your incompetence has made my friends in Chicago unhappy, and they expect you to correct the situation."

He explained what had transpired since Cornell Jackson's body was discovered and the events leading to the charges against Alessio.

"We believe the DA has evidence some of my people were involved in the assault of the Pryor woman—the most damaging being the woman has already identified Messina as one of her attackers. I expect you to make sure she doesn't testify, but I don't want her hurt. We have enough problems with the cops as it is. Just make sure she knows what will happen to her if she testifies in court. I'll leave the details to you."

Romano pushed a manilla envelope towards the gray-haired man. Inside was a brief bio and photo of Katy. Also included was the address where she lived, the name and address of the real estate company, and the names and pictures of her three employees.

Romano stood. "This job is between you and me. So keep your mouth shut and do it right this time, or Chicago will be very unhappy with you."

The gray-haired man gave a curt nod but said nothing. It was just dumb luck Jackson's body was found at that farm. He'd never failed to deliver on any of his assignments until now. But the truth was the job wasn't clean, and he owned that.

~~~~

Katy was buried in paperwork at her office late the following afternoon when her secretary, Judy Hunter, knocked on her door.

Judy was in her late fifties and had lived in Charleston all her life. She was what you might call an aging southern bell, her accent thick—just like her makeup. Like many women in small companies like Katy's, Judy took care of everything except the actual selling. Katy often made it clear Judy was the one that kept the company afloat.

"Come on in," Katy said.

Judy stuck her head in Katy's office. "You got a call on line one."

"Who is it?"
~~~~

"It's a Mrs. Phillips, and she's asking about our Buckley Lane listing on James Island. She's at the property and said it's just what she's looking for."

Katy checked her calendar. It was almost four o'clock. "Ask her if I can meet her there tomorrow at noon."

"I don't think that's going to work. The woman said she's flying back to Nashville first thing tomorrow morning."

The house was priced at $750,000 and was one of their best properties. "All right," Katy said and punched line one. "Good afternoon, Mrs. Phillips. This is Katy Pryor. I understand you're interested in our Buckley Lane listing."

"Yes, I'm here now and very interested. What is the asking price?"

"Seven hundred and fifty thousand," Katy replied, "and it's located in one of the most desirable communities on the island. I can be there in about a half-hour if that works for you."

"That would be great. I'm sorry about the rush, but I have a flight home tomorrow morning."

"I understand," Katy said. "I'll be there shortly."

Katy hung up the phone and told Judy she'd be back at the office no later than 6:00 pm and to go ahead and close up at 5:00 pm.

"I've got a ton of work to catch up on," Judy said, "and planned on staying late today. Plus, Jim has a business dinner and won't be home until nine."

"Are you sure?" Katy asked.

"Yes. I'll give you a call and lock up before I leave."

Katy thanked Judy and left for the showing.

The traffic was a nightmare, and it was approaching 5:00 by the time she got to the house. A car was parked in the driveway, and she pulled in next to it. Carrying her briefcase, Katy exited the Caprice just as a woman appeared from around the side of the house.

"Hello there," the woman called out. "You must be Ms. Pryor. I was admiring the house and noticed there's a dock. My husband loves to fish."

"Wonderful," Katy said, "Come with me, and I'll show you the inside of the house."

Katy opened the lockbox and removed the house key. She noticed the woman had stopped some ten to fifteen feet behind her. The woman was dressed in a white blouse under a blue wool blazer with a matching skirt. A scarf was tied around her neck, and she wore knee-length black leather boots.

Strange outfit for Charleston in July, Katy thought.

She used the key to open the front door and walked into the house, placing her briefcase on a table in the foyer. The woman followed her—still keeping her distance.

The family who'd lived in the house had moved out the previous week. While Katy always preferred to present her listings furnished, the home was immaculate and showed well.

"If you follow me, I'd be happy to show you around," Katy offered.

The woman turned toward the fireplace on the far wall and said, "Thank you, but I'd rather do that myself if it's all right with you. I'm sure I'll have questions for you."

The request wasn't unusual for many of her clients.

"Take as much time as you like," Katy said. "I'll wait here, and then we can see the upstairs."

The woman walked through the living room and entered the formal dining room. A moment later, Katy could hear the sound of her boots on the kitchen floor. The Phillips woman returned to the living room a few minutes later. Her eyes still set on the fireplace, she said, "What a lovely home. This is just perfect. Can you show me the upstairs?"

"Of course, if you'll just follow me. I think you'll love the layout."

Katy started up the stairs, hearing the click-clack of boots on the hardwood stairs following her. She was about halfway up when something shoved her violently in the center of her back, causing her to fall face-first hard onto the wooden stairs. Pain shot through her like a lightning bolt. Stunned, Katy tried to get up but was pushed back down. She felt an arm go around the front of her neck and another behind the back. It felt like a vice as the gray-haired man tightened his grip—the pressure cutting off the flow of blood to the carotid artery. It was only a matter of five to ten seconds before Katy lost consciousness.

The gray-haired man, wearing black surgical gloves, dragged her down the stairs. He then removed three heavy plastic zip ties from the inside pocket of the blazer. The first tie was used to tightly secure Katy's ankles and the second to firmly bind her hands behind her. After placing her in a sitting position at the base of the stairs, he looped the third tie around the one binding her hands, pulling her tightly against one of the heavy wooden banisters. Knowing he only had 25 to 30 seconds before the

Pryor woman regained consciousness, he retrieved her briefcase and removed her cell phone. He returned to the stairs and bent down on one knee—his face now level with hers.

It was only a matter of seconds before Katy moved, and her eyes fluttered. She felt confused and bewildered. Then came a flash of pain where her forehead had slammed into one of the wooden stairs. *Where am I*, she thought, and then it came back rushing to her—the Phillips woman, the property on James Island, falling hard on the stairs.

She heard a voice—deep and guttural—an aura of menace about it. You could almost smell it. "What a lovely house you have here, but I don't think it's going to work for me."

Katy opened her eyes and found herself staring into the face of the woman she was showing the house to. But the face looked different, and then there were the eyes—hollow, black, and foreboding, like portals to something dark and ungodly. Katy tried to move, but the plastic ties cut deep into her wrists and feet. She tried to turn away, but the person in front of her, whoever it was, grabbed a handful of hair and yanked her head back. Katy saw the broad-bladed knife slowly waving back and forth only inches from her face. She felt the flat blade of the knife touch her forehead, slide over her right eye, down the cheek, and stop at the side of her neck.

"Make a sound, and I will cut you. Understand?"

Katy nodded her head rapidly.

"Good," the voice said, "you need to listen carefully. If you testify in a particular court case, I will come back for you and end your life in a very unpleasant way. I will do the same to your secretary, Judy Hunter, and your two young agents, Susan and Lily. Do you understand?"

Katy again nodded.

"Good," the voice said and dropped Katy's cell phone on the hardwood floor and repeatedly smashed it with the butt of the hunting knife until it was in pieces.

"Oh dear, I believe I broke it," he said grimly.

The gray-haired man stood, pointed the knife at Katy, and said, "You seem like a smart girl. If you open your mouth in court or tell anyone what happened here today, I will end you and your three friends. I'd rather not do that. When the carotid artery is cut, blood tends to spray out like a firehose. It can get so messy."

He turned and left.

Katy felt a wave of nausea wash over her and started to shake. She found it hard to catch her breath. Warm wetness spread underneath her as her bladder emptied. She couldn't control her shaking—the words 'I will end you' repeating over and over in her mind until she slumped forward and passed out.

~~~~

Judy had just finished assembling packets for all the company's active listings when she saw it was already 7:00 pm. She hadn't heard from Katy, which was unusual. Judy returned to her desk, called Katy's cell number, and was surprised when it went directly to voicemail. Maybe Katy went straight home after her showing, but why was her phone going to voicemail? Judy made
~~~~

several more calls, each ending the same way. All her messages remained unanswered.

Judy closed the office and drove home—trying Katy again in her car. No luck.

It was 8:00 by the time she made it home and got settled. Still nothing from Katy. Judy made another call ending in the same result. Now her concern heightened even more. Katy had been gone over four hours for a showing that should have lasted no more than thirty minutes. Something was wrong. Her husband was still at his business dinner, so she decided to phone Vince.

She made the call.

He answered, and Judy said, "Vince, this is Judy Hunter."

"Hey, Judy, what's up?"

"I'm getting worried about Katy. She left the office this afternoon to show a house on James Island. She's been gone over four hours and isn't returning any of my calls. That's not like her."

Vince felt a twitch of angst. "Did she go alone?"

"Yes."

"What's the address?" Vince demanded.

"Sixty Buckley Lane on James island," Judy quickly answered.

"Thanks, Judy; I'm heading out there now."

"Let me know what going on," Judy said, but Vince had already disconnected the call.

Vince grabbed the keys to the VW and left the duplex. He punched the Buckley address into google maps and made it out to James Island in about twenty minutes. Vince approached the house and noticed Katy's Caprice was still parked in the driveway. He pulled in and jumped out of the VW, leaving its door wide open.

Vince ran to the front door, opened it, and froze when he saw Katy slumped against the stairwell. He caught a glimpse of the plastic ties, removed his pocketknife, and began cutting her free.

"Christ, Katy. What happened?"

Katy blinked several times before finally opening her eyes. She simply stared at Vince but said nothing—withdrawing into herself. Vince had seen the same look in the shell-shocked faces of soldiers in the mountains of Afghanistan and the deserts of Yemen. It was like a switch flipped. Vince's jaw clenched, and his muscles contracted—he felt his whole body transform into Raiders mode—*Never quit. Never surrender. Never fail.*

His voice firm but controlled, Vince repeated, "What happened?"

Katy began to find focus, and she whispered, "Vince."

"Who did this?" Vince asked, his voice more urgent.

Katy shook her head but said nothing.

Vince removed his cell phone and was about to dial 911 when Katy said, "No!"

"Oh, Jesus," Vince muttered. It was now clear that whoever attacked Katy had to be sent by Romano to stop her from testifying in the Messina case.

"All right. Can you walk?"

Katy nodded, and Vince helped her up. She was unsteady as they walked to the front door. Vince saw her briefcase on the table in the foyer and grabbed it before leaving the house. He kicked the door shut behind him. It took some doing, but he finally got Katy in the front seat of the VW. Her face was void of color, and she was unresponsive when Vince asked her to buckle her seatbelt. He reached over and fastened it. Before leaving, he opened her briefcase, got her car keys, and used the remote to lock the Caprice.

No way was Katy going back to her apartment. Vince thought about taking her to Ryan's place but realized that wouldn't work either. He needed a safe house—somewhere unknown to Coppola, Romano, and the animal who threatened her. The choice was obvious. His mother's house.

Thirty minutes later, Vince helped Katy out of the car, and they made their way to his mom's front door. He tried opening it, but it was locked, and he didn't have his key. He knocked loudly, and a moment later, Shelly appeared. Seeing her son, she smiled and was about to say something when she saw Katy. Her smile disappeared. "Oh, Lord."

"Mom, Katy and I need to stay here for a few days."

"Of course. What in the world happened?"

Vince ignored the question and helped Katy down the hall and into one of Shelly's spare bedrooms. He pulled back the covers and got her in bed. "Stay here and rest. I'll be right back."

He turned to leave but heard Katy call out, "Vince, you can't tell anyone what that man did to me." Vince said nothing. There was an urgency in her voice when she said, "Please."

Vince understood. "Right," he said. "Stay there. I'll be back in a minute."

Shelly was waiting outside the bedroom door, arms crossed over her chest. "What's going on, Son?"

Vince didn't want to lie to his mother but knew he couldn't tell Shelly what had happened to Katy. He got away with a half-truth by saying, "Katy had a fall while she was working and hit her head. She's a little nauseous, and I'm concerned she might have a mild concussion. I didn't want her at her apartment by herself. I'm sure she'd be okay in a day or two."

Katy seemed a bit more cogent when Vince returned to the bedroom with a glass of water. He placed the water on the nightstand and sat on the side of the bed. His eyes were kind, but his voice was firm. "Now, tell me what happened."

It was apparent the ordeal had completely drained Katy. Still unhinged, she did her best to explain bits and pieces of what occurred at the James Island house.

Vince listened patiently. "You told me the Phillips woman attacked you."

"Yes, but I don't think she was a woman."

It was now clear to Vince he was dealing with a professional—one without a conscience. Someone skillful at disguises but predatory enough to intimidate Katy into refusing to testify in the Messina case. Vince knew men in the service like that. These men were outliners who remained in the military because of some deep-seated addiction to violence.

"I want you to rest now," Vince said, his voice carrying a gentle tone. "Try to get some sleep. I promise I'm not going anywhere."

He sat in an overstuffed sofa chair in the corner of the room. Katy lay motionless on the bed; her eyes riveted on the slow-moving blades of the ceiling fan above her. She stayed that way for about twenty minutes until her eyes closed, and she fell into a deep sleep. Soon the nightmare came. Dark and murky water swirled around her until a hand reached out and began lifting her up. Suddenly, the smiling face of the Phillips woman appeared—until it began to contort into something twisted and unholy. Its eye showed blood red. Its garish mouth opened wide, displaying rows of razor-sharp teeth. The hand let her go, and she felt herself falling into blackness.

Vince left the bedroom and quietly slipped out of the front door. He called Ryan and told him Katy had fallen at work. He was concerned she had a mild concussion and, to be on the safe side, he would be staying with her at his mom's house for the next few days.

Vince had memorized the phone numbers of four of his closest Raider brothers, all of whom had pulled the pin on active duty within a year of his own Expiration of Term of Service (ETS). He removed his cell phone and opened an app called Phoner. The application allowed an individual to call or text with complete autonomy by randomly creating a second phone number that could not be directly associated with the owner's actual number.

Two of his brothers resided in California, one in Jacksonville, Florida, and one outside Atlanta, Georgia. He chose the two closest to Charleston and sent the following text to each of them:

Need help. Light action required. Wolf Track Tavern, 1807 Parsonage Rd, Charleston. Tomorrow 6:00 pm. Drive. No fly. No cards. Vince. SF

Vince had no doubt both men would be at the bar the next day. The meaning of the phrase *"action required"* was clear—be mission ready. He returned to the bedroom and remained in the sofa chair, watching Katy and catching what sleep he could until early the following morning.

CHAPTER 26

SHELLY WAS HAVING toast and coffee when Vince joined her in the kitchen Thursday morning.

"How's Katy?" she asked.

"She's still sleeping."

"Do you think she needs to see a doctor?"

"I'll see how she feels when she wakes up," Vince answered.

"All right, sweetheart. I need to leave for work. Please call me and let me know how she's feeling."

As Shelly was leaving, she stopped and turned back toward Vince. She'd sensed a subtle change in him—a hardness he rarely displayed around her.

"Are you sure you're okay, honey?"

"I'll be fine, Mom. I promise to call."

Katy slept until almost 10:00 am. While it was clear she was still profoundly disturbed, she did seem more coherent than the night before.

Vince helped Katy to the kitchen table and made scrambled eggs and toast. He waited for her to eat until it became clear she'd eaten all she could—which was very little. He asked her if she felt up to telling him more about what happened yesterday.

Katy nodded.

"Good," Vince continued, "You said the person that threatened you was a man. What exactly did he say?"

"He said that if I testified in the Messina case, he would kill my three employees and me. There was something perverse about the man. I don't know if that's the right word. I guess maybe coldblooded. Either way, there's no doubt in my mind he'd do exactly what he said he would."

"Did he hurt you in any way?"

"Only when he pushed me down on the stairs and tied me up. I don't remember him actually hitting me. He did threaten me with a knife but never used it."

Vince had several more questions for Katy. Many things were still vague to her, but she did her best to answer them. When Vince was satisfied he'd get little more from Katy, he cleared the table and walked to the kitchen sink when she stopped him.

"Vince, you have to promise me you won't tell your mom or Ryan."

"I promise. Now, I want you to rest. Mom is getting back from work around four o'clock. When she does, I'm going to drive out to your place to pick up some clothes and makeup for you. I also want to stop by Ryan's to get some of my stuff."

Katy did nap for an hour or two giving Vince time to figure out how to keep her safe. He knew that even if Katy didn't testify, she still posed a threat to the Organization, and bad things often happen to people who are a threat to the mob. In many ways, the mafia operates like any large business. Their decisions are made based on the potential profit and loss expected from those decisions. Somehow Vince and his Raider brothers would have to do something to make the Organization realize that killing Katy would be a greater risk than allowing her to live. The problem was what to do to make that scenario work.

Vince had asked Katy what she wanted from her apartment.

"I need my computer, tennis shoes, some slacks, blouses, underwear, and makeup. That should do it for now."

As expected, Shelly got home around 4:15 that afternoon. Vince left at 4:30 and made the short ten-minute drive to Katy's apartment. He packed up what she would need and left for the Citadel Mall. The mall has a shop called Clair's that sells various jewelry and tourist goods. Vince bought a plastic replica of a South Carolina license plate. It resembles the real thing with the letters spelling out "I LOVE SC" on the plate. He left for Ryan's place, arriving 15 minutes later. Vince hoped his friend wouldn't be there. He knew Ryan would question him further about Katy, and he didn't want to go there. However, as he approached the duplex, he saw Ryan's Silverado parked in front of it.

Vince parked the VW behind Ryan's truck and walked to the door. It was locked, and he knocked. A moment later, Ryan opened the door and said, "Hello there, stranger."

Vince walked past him.

"Hey, buddy. I just need to grab a few things and get back to my mom's house."

Ryan said nothing.

It took a few minutes for Vince to pack up what he needed into a small backpack and slip it on. When he left his bedroom, Ryan was waiting for him by the kitchen counter. He wasn't smiling.

Vince was heading to the door when he said, "I'll give you a call and let you know how things are going."

After over twenty years of friendship, the boys had no trouble reading each other, and Ryan knew there were things Vince wasn't telling him about what happened to Katy.

Before Vince could make it to the door, he heard Ryan call out, "Hey, Vince." Vince turned, and Ryan asked suspiciously, "What's really going on?"

Growing up, the boys had rarely kept secrets from one another. Even though Vince knew he couldn't tell Ryan everything, it was clear he owed his friend some level of the truth.

Vince returned to where Ryan was standing, removed his backpack, and placed it on the floor next to him.

"All right," Vince finally said, "There are some things that have happened that I just can't tell you about. You're my best friend, but you're going to have to trust me on this. You can't be involved."

It was clear Ryan wasn't happy. But he knew Vince well enough to understand there must be good reasons to keep him in the dark.

A moment of silence persisted until Ryan begrudgingly said, "Okay, I'll give you this one, but you need to promise you'll let me know if I can help."

Vince glanced at his watch. He had less than ten minutes to get to the Wolf Track Tavern to meet his Raider brothers.

"I promise, but I need to go," he said. "I know you're pissed, but thanks for understanding."

He was almost to the door when Vince heard Ryan say, "Just don't get yourself killed."

Without turning, Vince gave Ryan the thumbs up.

~~~~

Vince arrived at the tavern at 6:10 pm. It was slow at that time of the evening. Most of the tables were empty, and only half the barstools taken. There were two pool tables and a pinball machine in the back. Several TVs were mounted on the walls televising various sports shows. A string of Christmas lights hung behind the bar above the rows of liquor bottles. The place was trying hard to be a sport's bar, but in reality, it was only a notch or two above a dive bar—which suited Vince just fine.

The light was dim, but Vince immediately spotted his two comrades, Billy Hawk and Joe Knight. Joe waved at him, caught the waitress's attention, and ordered a beer for Vince.

Billy Hawk was a full-blooded Native American born and raised on the Brighton Seminole Indian Reservation in southcentral Florida. He was a good student, notwithstanding the below-average schools on the reservation. William
~~~~

Nighthawk was his birth name until his father shortened their surname to Hawk almost twenty years ago to blend in with the white population and culture in the area. It was at that time the tribe started the Brighton Casino. Billy's father was employed there since it began operating in 2002 and was now one of the casino's vice presidents. As he got older, Billy wasn't pleased with the change of his last name and tried hard to hold onto his Seminole culture. He was disappointed that many of his people had moved away from their heritage toward the world of the white man. It was a confusing and ambiguous time for Billy, and it surprised no one that he enlisted in the Marines Corps the day after he graduated from high school.

Billy's narrow forehead, raised cheekbones, jet black hair, and brownish skin left no question he was a Native American. And just like Vince, Billy's years in the Corps, especially those as a Raider, had given him the confidence he lacked growing up on the reservation.

Joe Knight was the complete opposite of Hawk. He was five inches taller than Billy, his hair blond and long, and his Scandinavian facial features evident. He grew up in a well-to-do county club family in a suburb of Atlanta. Joe's grades in high school were good, but his skills on the basketball court were even better. In addition to his prowess on the hardwood, he had developed a computer expertise that was nothing short of astonishing. While Joe's parents could have paid for just about any college or university, he decided on Georgia Southern University primarily because they offered him a partial basketball scholarship. He spent a year at the university but became disillusioned with the grind of basketball practices and college life in general. The summer after his freshman year, and against his parents' wishes, Joe enlisted in the Marines.

Hawk and Knight, like other Marines, are known for their strength, endurance, and various other skills—especially the MCMAP (Marine Corps Martial Arts Program.) The MCMAP program combines close-quarter weapon use, Brazilian Jujitsu, Judo, kickboxing, and Krav Maga, the standard of the Israeli Defense Forces. Jujitsu, in particular, taught the use of critical pressure points that could disable or even render an opponent unconscious.

Like other forms of martial arts, Marines are issued a colored belt designating their level of proficiency. All Marine Raiders have an upper degree brown belt, and many achieved black belt status. Despite his size, Billy had a level three black belt and was the most competent in hand-to-hand combat in their unit.

Billy and Joe were seated in a booth against the far wall away from the other patrons. Vince hadn't seen his friends in almost a year, and despite the circumstances, it felt good to be with them again. Vince made it to their table, and after handshakes and embraces, he took a seat across from his brothers.

The waitress brought the beer, and Vince turned to Billy. "Hey, chief, how's Jacksonville?"

"The city's not bad," Billy answered. "I've been working at the Volvo dealership for the past year and doing pretty well. The clientele is decent, and they've got money to spend. Can't complain."

"How about you, surfer boy?" Vince asked Joe.

"I'm back in Atlanta working with my dad at his chain of sporting goods stores. Dad's mellowed and pretty much lets me handle the three stores he gave me to manage. Like Billy here, I can't complain."

Vince smirked. "Any women in your lives I should know about?"

Billy and Joe smiled at each other. Billy was the first to answer. "I've been seeing a girl who lives in my apartment complex. She's a lot of fun. Not sure what, if anything, will come of it."

Vince asked Joe if he'd met anyone special.

Joe smiled and said, "They're all special. Plus, I'm a confirmed bachelor, at least for now."

Vince updated his friend on his new apartment and the Maritime Interdiction Agent job he'd just landed.

Billy asked about Katy, and Vince explained they had recently split but were still best of friends. "I guess neither of us could handle the marriage thing. As a matter of fact, Katy is the main reason I asked you two here."

Billy and Joe leaned forward, and Vince explained how the whole sequence of events had led to Katy's life being threatened. It took him over a half-hour to cover everything, from the fiasco with the Honda to the second time Katy was attacked.

When Vince was finished, Billy whispered, "Jesus."

The three men were quiet until Joe asked, "So, read us in. What's the plan?"

"Like I said, the only thing I'm sure of is that the attack on Katy was ordered by Frank Romano or Michael Coppola. Even if she doesn't testify, I doubt she'll be safe until we do something that would make killing Katy riskier to them than letting her live."

"Wait a minute, Vince," Joe interrupted. "You said this Coppola guy reports to Romano, and he wouldn't do anything big without the okay from his boss. It sounds like Coppola is the low man on the totem pole. Sorry about that, Billy."

"That's all right," Billy replied. "And I have to agree with Joe. The Seminole have a saying, 'Cut off the head of a snake, and the body withers away.'"

"So you're both saying if we get Romano to back off Katy," Vince offered, "Coppola and the person that threatened Katy become irrelevant."

"Exactly," Joe said, "but the problem is: how do we get Romano to back off."

Vince answered, "Remember that crime reporter at our local newspaper I told you about?"

Billy and Joe said nothing, waiting for more.

"Right. The reporter told me Romano flies to Chicago the first Friday of every month to see his boss. While he's up there, he visits his daughter at Northwestern University."

"I see where you're going," Joe said, "Romano threatens Katy; we threaten his daughter. It sounds like this Romano guy is pretty high up on the Mafia food chain. Are you sure you want to get into a pissing contest with him?"

"If we do this right," Vince answered, "It could work."

"Could work, or will work?" Joe questioned.

Vince shot back, "If we make it convincing enough, it'll work. There may be something else we can do, but this is all I have so far."

Joe nodded.

"Okay, Vince," Billy said, "we've got your back."

"When is this going to go down?" Joe asked.

"That reporter told me Romano leaves his office Monday through Friday at seven in the evening," Vince answered. "And he rarely, if ever varies this schedule. He's only got a few employees, and they're all gone by five o'clock. That gives us a two-hour window, and we'll hit him at around six o'clock tomorrow evening. Let's plan on meeting here in the parking lot at five. I've got a storage unit where we can pick up anything else we need. His import business is called AC Global Imports. It's in a North Charleston industrial park, and I've already reconned the area. His place is on a cul-de-sac in a new part of the industrial park. There are some occupied buildings and several vacant lots and partially built buildings on the street."

Vince glanced at his watch. It was already 7:30 pm.

"Okay, guys, I got to go. But now you know what we're facing. So, like Billy said, let's see if we can come up with something else that will neutralize Romano."

Vince tossed $30 on the table and headed to the exit, followed by his two brothers. As soon as they left the bar, Vince stopped and said, "I assume you're mission ready, and your weapons are packed."

They nodded, and Joe added, "You said light mission-ready, right?"

"Yes," Vince answered. "I've got everything else we'll need. Joe, what are you driving?"

"A white Lexus RX."

"How about you, Billy?" Vince asked.

"A Ford Taurus."

"All right," Vince said, "We'll meet here in the parking lot at five tomorrow. Billy, we'll take your Taurus."

Billy nodded.

"Where are you guys staying?" Vince asked.

"Nowhere yet," Joe answered. "You said no cards."

"How about you, Billy?"

"Same."

"Good. There are a few small motels about twenty or twenty-five miles south on Highway 17. They're not your Hilton or Marriot, but they'll take cash. Use one of your alternate IDs."

Billy and Joe got into their cars and were about to leave when they saw Vince slide into the front seat of the VW.

Joe pulled up beside him, rolled down his window, and said, "Nice ride there, Vince."

"Tomorrow, five o'clock," Vince said with a smile.

~~~~

On his way back to his mom's house, Vince racked his brain, searching for another solution that would guarantee Katy's safety. He could think of nothing and began to berate himself
~~~~

for all he had done to put her life in danger. The whole thing felt like one of those cheap 1940s gangster movies with the mobsters in long black coats carrying Tommy guns.

When Vince made it back to his mom's house, he found Shelly and Katy in the kitchen having coffee.

"Well, the parodical son finally returns," Shelly said. "I'll get you a cup of coffee. Just made it."

Vince held up the suitcase and backpack.

"Coffee sounds good, but let me put these away first."

Vince put Katy's suitcase in her room and had just dropped off his backpack in his room when he saw Shelly standing in the doorway.

"What's really going on with Katy? I asked her several times about her fall, and she never really answered me. She kept changing the subject."

"I wouldn't worry, Mom. I think she's still shaken up. She'll be confused for the next few days. She might even have a mild concussion. I'll watch her. Don't worry."

"Well, you know I will," Shelly said.

"I know," Vince replied with a smile.

Vince and Shelly returned to the kitchen and joined Katy. Vince poured a cup of coffee for himself, and the three of them talked for over an hour.

Looking at the kitchen clock, Shelly said, "I better get some sleep. Irene and I are off work tomorrow, and we're going with two of our friends to Magnolia Plantation first thing in the morning."

Vince shook his head. "Mom, how many times have you been there?"

"I don't remember. Maybe two or three, but that's not the point. It's always fun. There're guided tours where the people that work there dress up like they did in the Revolutionary War. Plus, we're going to have lunch afterward. I get to catch up on all the gossip."

Vince knew he would need to leave to meet Billy and Joe at around four-thirty and asked Shelly what time she expected to be back home.

"Oh, I don't know. Probably when we get kicked out of the restaurant. I'd say between two and three."

"All right. Have fun." Vince was relieved, knowing his mom would be home well before he had to leave for the Wolf Track Tavern.

Katy wanted to rest. She thanked Shelly for everything, and Vince walked her back to her room.

When they got there, Vince asked how she really felt.

"I'm feeling better but still a little shaky. But I'm even more convinced I'm not going to testify, and I want you to promise me again you won't call the police or tell Shelly and Ryan about what really happened."

Vince promised and left for his own room. Later that evening, he returned to Katy's room and again sat with her the rest of the night.

CHAPTER 27

THE FOLLOWING MORNING, Vince left Katy's room at 6:00 am. He'd packed his running shoes and planned on upping his jaunt to ten miles. He took off through the predawn grays of morning.

Vince returned from his run an hour and twenty minutes later and found his mom having orange juice and toast in the kitchen.

"Good morning, Son. How was your jog?"

He always got a kick out of Shelly, calling his seven-minute mile runs a mere jog.

"Get yourself some coffee and breakfast," she continued. "I have to finish getting dressed. I leave for Irene's in about fifteen minutes. Don't forget we have our little adventure today."

Vince again asked her what time she'd be back.

"Like I told you, I'll be back probably by two o'clock but no later than three."

That again helped relieve Vince's concern about the rest of the day, knowing he'd to able to meet Hawk and Knight in the Wolf Track Tavern's parking lot at 5:00 that afternoon.

Shelly left at 8:00 am. Katy finally woke up a little before 9:30 am. Vince made her a light breakfast and asked her how she felt. It was clear Katy was still nervous. The nightmares of her attack had returned, but she didn't want to talk about them.

They both spent the next few hours on their computers. Katy worked on her business, and Vince researched what he could find on Frank Romano and the mafia in Charleston and Chicago. Around two o'clock that afternoon, Katy wanted to get some fresh air, so they walked around the neighborhood. When they returned, Shelly was back from her trip.

"How was it?" Vince asked.

"It's always fun, and I got some juicy tidbits about some of the people I work with at the library."

"That's nice," Vince said, faining a smile.

"How's Katy doing?" Shelly asked.

"A little better, but she still gets confused sometimes. She had more nightmares last night. We just need to give her some time."

"What do you want for dinner?" Shelly asked.

"Don't worry about me, Mom. I was thinking of going to the Citadel Mall. I need to buy another suit and some clothes to wear to my new job. I also want to stop by Ryan's for a while. I'll probably get home late and make something myself."

Shelly smiled. "Since when did you start cooking? I'll make you a good dinner and put it in the icebox."

"Thanks, Mom."

Vince left at 4:30 pm and drove to the tavern, arriving at 5:00 pm. By then, the weather had changed, and the sky turned the color of slate. The wind had picked up, and dark clouds began to roll in off the ocean, bringing the first drops of rain. Bits of paper and empty fast-food wrappers danced across the road.

Billy's and Joe's cars were parked at the far end of the lot. Joe was sitting with Billy in the Taurus; both dressed in black cargo pants, long-sleeved black T-shirts, and tan leather combat boots. Vince parked next to him, grabbed the bag carrying the fake license plate, and got into the back seat of the Taurus.

"Everything good?" Vince asked.

"All good," Joe answered, and Billy nodded.

Vince confirmed both of them had already checked out of their motel and instructed Billy to take a left out of the lot and follow Ashley River Road to his storage locker. Once they arrived, he unlocked his unit and raised the garage-type door. Vince removed a map he'd drawn of the industrial park cul-de-sac where Romano's business was located. Billy and Joe huddled together, and Vince began explaining the diagram.

"Romano's building is in a new section of the industrial park, and in addition to his, there are only six other completed buildings on the street. Most of the other lots are vacant or under construction." He pointed out Romano's business and moved on. "There are two vacant lots to his right, one under construction to his left, and another on being built directly across from Romano's building." He pointed out a building across from Romano's and continued, "That's where we'll park and gear up."

"Wait a minute," Joe interrupted, "all those finished businesses will have security cameras, and there's no way Billy's car and plate won't be recorded."

"You're right," Vince said, "but put that aside for now. What weapons and tactical gear did you bring?"

"Standard light-mission, just like you told us," Billy answered.

"Just in case you forgot anything," Vince said. He unlocked the combination padlock on the steel cabinet and swung the heavy door open.

"You son-of-a-bitch," Joe said.

"Christ, it looks like an armory in there!" Billy added.

"Hell," Vince said, "you guys know when you're in Afghanistan, and someone is constantly trying to kill you, you feel naked without gunning up. Plus, all of that stuff was bought legally."

Hanging on hooks in the back of the locker was an AK-47 machine gun and two Glock 19s. There were also two heavy-duty tactical belts with double-pocketed X-26 Serpa® holster slots for the Glock and a Blackhawk Taser®, ammunition pouches, and other combat accessories.

A lightweight Kevlar® vest and several types of broad-bladed knives hung the sides of the locker. Packs of 9mm bullets, clips, and a box of 150-decibel flash-bang grenades sat on one of the locker shelves. A few scrapbooks containing photos and other memorabilia from Vince's years in the Marines rested on another. Leaning against the side of the locker was a 40-pound steel battering ram.

"Take what you need," he said.

Billy and Joe grabbed a box of 9mm bullets. Joe pointed to the Kevlar® vest and asked if he could use the one in the locker.

"Sure," Vince replied and gestured to the brown canvas bag resting at the base of the locker. "I've already got everything I'll need in there, including the flash-bangs. These have a three-second delay, so be careful." Vince picked up his bag and the battering ram and put them on the table next to the locker. "Anything else you guys need?"

"No, I'm good-to-go," Joe said. Billy nodded his agreement.

Vince shed his pants and shoes, changing into black pants and high-top leather boots. After closing and locking the garage door behind him, Vince deposited his bag and ram in the trunk of the Taurus and said, "All right, let's rock and roll."

Halfway down I-526 on the way to the industrial park, Vince removed the replica of the I LOVE SC license plate and told Billy to pull off the highway onto the berm. He handed Billy a Phillips head and the replica plate and said, "Replace your rear license plate with this one."

Billy held it out for Joe to see, and they both smiled. "You got it," Billy said and replaced the plate.

It was 6:05 pm by the time they arrived at the industrial park. Billy drove down the cul-de-sac and backed into the rock-covered driveway of the partially constructed building across from Romano's business. Both Romano's Escalade and Alessio's Charger were parked in front of the building. The rain had now intensified as Billy popped the trunk. The three of them removed their gear, entered the building, and began suiting up.

Vince removed his AK-47 and double-checked it was operational with precise movements. There were a series of clicks and clacks, and he was satisfied in a matter of seconds.

Joe asked Vince if he knew the layout of Romano's building.

"No, not completely. Most of the building is taken up by a truck port in the rear and space to store whatever its company's product. I don't know the actual inside layout, but most of these small industrial buildings are pretty much the same. They usually have a small reception area in front with a few offices and a restroom down a hall leading to the truck port area. Nothing we haven't faced before. We'll monitor and adjust."

"So, what's the plan?" Joe asked.

Before he answered, Vince removed three full-face black stocking caps, giving Billy and Joe one each. He did the same with three flash-bang grenades.

Vince took out the map he'd made of the area and began, "We'll cross the two vacant lots and approach the rear of the building. I'm assuming the truck port entrance will be locked. If so, we'll move to the front of the building. Most of these businesses have reinforced wood doors. If the door is locked, which I assume it will be, I'll use the battering ram. Billy, you're point. Clear the reception room, and Joe and I will follow you in. We'll proceed down the hall until we identify the office Romano is in. Whoever's there will be armed and aware of what's going down, so stay frosty."

Billy and Joe nodded, and Vince said, "Any questions?" There were none. The sound of thunder rumbled above them, and he added, "Okay, boys, it's time to dance with the devil."

They moved quickly and low to the ground through the two mud-covered vacant lots, making it to the rear of the building in about ten seconds.

Billy crossed the back of the loading dock and carefully tried the back door. It was locked. The three of them moved to the front of the building and found that door was also locked. Vince shouldered his AK-47, took a position in front of the entrance, and gave a hand signal he would breach the door. He gestured for Billy to enter first, followed by Joe. Vince swung the 40-pound ram two times before connecting with the door. It splintered but remained secure. He tried again, this time knocking it partially open. Billy kicked it down, crouched, and entered—his Glock extended, his elbow slightly bent. He signaled the reception room was clear and moved forward down the hallway, with Joe and Vince following close behind.

A second later, Alessio's huge head and hand appeared in the doorway. Billy saw the .38 and dove to his left just as the big man got off two rounds—the second hitting Joe directly in the chest. He was thrown back, landing hard on the floor. Billy fired his Glock—the bullet ripped through Alessio's forearm, knocking the .38 from his hand. Alessio stumbled back inside the office. Vince removed the flash-bang grenade, and Billy did the same. They both pulled the pin, tossed them into the room, and covered their ears. Two seconds later, two bright flashes and deafening explosions erupted. Vince stuck his AK-47 around the side of the office door and let go with two short bursts into the ceiling.

The flash-bangs served their purpose, and when the two of them rushed in, Romano and Alessio were partially blinded and disoriented from the blasts.

Romano had moved away from his desk and was now at the far end of his office. Although still dazed, he held a gun in his right hand. Vince crouched, crossed the room, and kicked the pistol from Romano's hand. Another kick to his stomach, and a vicious punch to his head, had Romano on the floor. Vince put the gun to his head and shouted, "Move, and you die!"

Like Romano, Alessio was still in a fog from the explosions. Billy kicked him in the groin, causing the big man to scissor forward, grabbing his family jewels—just as Billy's muscle memory brought his knee straight up, connecting with Alessio's nose. An audible crack could be heard as the nose shattered. A wild punch from Alessio caught Billy in the chest, knocking him back into the wall. He recovered in time to see the giant coming toward him—his face bloodied, his arms outstretched. Ducking, Billy spun to his left and slammed his fist into the base of Alessio's right ear. The big man went down like a sack of rocks.

An eerie silence now filled the room as Billy and Vince's eyes met.

Vince pulled two black heavy-duty plastic ties from his belt and bound Romano's hands behind his back and to one of the legs of his heavy desk. At the same time, Billy dragged Alessio across the room, grabbed him under the arms, and threw him into a chair in front of Romano's desk. He tied each of Alessio's feet to the chair's rear legs and was trying to secure his hands together when Joe appeared at the office door. He leaned against the door jamb—his left hand holding his chest, his right gripping a knife.

Joe surveyed the situation and said, "Which one shot me?"

"This asshole," Billy said, who now had Alessio's right hand behind him but was struggling with the left.

Joe took a step toward and brought the butt of his MK-43 knife down hard to the back of Alessio's head. The blow stunned him enough for Billy to tie both hands together behind him. He used another plastic tie to affix Alessio's hands to one of the metal slats at the back of the chair.

Now that both men were under control, Vince said. "Here's how it's going to be."

A slight smile materialized on Romano's face, and he grumbled, "I know who you are, and you have no idea who you're dealing with."

Before he could say another word, Vince pressed the barrel of his AK-47 hard against the side of Romano's head, silencing him.

"And I know who you are," Vince responded. "But, trust me, you have no idea who we are. Now keep your mouth shut and listen. Katy Pryor will not testify against your friend here, and she will not be harmed by your people or anyone else in any way. And I mean in any way. If she gets hit by a car, trips on the sidewalk, or even gets a hangnail, we'll pay a visit to your daughter, Teresa, at Northwestern, and she will pay the price."

Romano's face twisted in rage, and his eyes filled with hate, but he said nothing.

Vince shot a glance at Joe and pointed at Romano's desk. "Check the desk for weapons."

Still holding his chest, Joe knew the bullet had broken at least a few ribs, but the Kevlar® vest had saved his life. He checked under the desk and found the empty sleeve that had held Romano's gun. After checking all the drawers and finding no weapons, he noticed a laptop opened on the desk in front of him. It displayed a spreadsheet. He studied the spreadsheet, waved at Vince, and said, "Take a look at this."

Still holding his gun on Romano, Vince joined Joe at the desk. He first noticed a pile of handwritten slips next to an open computer displaying a spreadsheet. He studied the computer screen and whispered, "Son of a bitch. Well, look what we have here."

The spreadsheet identified several Charleston neighborhoods—each listing dollar amounts for drugs, prostitution, and other categories of criminal activities. A USB flash drive was in the side of the laptop. Joe downloaded the file.

Vince turned the computer around so Romano could see it and said, "I believe this changes things. If Ms. Pryor or anyone associated with her is hurt, we will still make your daughter pay. But now we have another insurance policy. Your computer will be put into a safety deposit box, and a copy of the flash drive given to a lawyer with instructions to send it to the FBI and Charleston's police if any of us are hurt. They will be thrilled to receive it, but that won't be your biggest problem. We'll also have a copy of the spreadsheet sent to Mr. Cataudella in Chicago. He'll be very unhappy with you, and I think you know what he'll do about it. But as long as Ms. Pryor and the rest of us remain safe, this will stay between you and me. We'll call it our insurance policy. Do you understand?"

Romano said nothing, but Vince could see the anxiety and fear spreading across his face. "Do you understand!" Vince repeated, and Romano gave a slight nod. Vince gestured to the door. "We're finished here." The three of them left the office.

Once out of the building, Vince grabbed the battering ram, and they made their way back through the vacant lots to the partly constructed site where they'd geared up. They all were soaked, their pants and boots covered in mud. Once they helped Joe remove his vest and the rest of his equipment, Vince and Billy shed their own. The gear was bagged and deposited in the trunk of the Taurus. Billy pulled out of the driveway, rocks peppering the bottom of his car like buckshot, and proceeded down the cul-da-sac, turning right toward the Industrial park's exit.

Since leaving Romano's office, no one had uttered a word. The adrenaline was still pumping.

"Hell of a job, guys," Vince said.

"You'd done the same for us," Billy answered. "Spiritus Invictus."

"Semper fi," Joe added.

Vince took the computer and flash drive from Joe and said, "When we get back to the tavern, I want both of you to head home. But on the way, lose your boots. Sole prints of our boots are all over Romano's office and the building where we got suited up. Billy, when you get back to Jacksonville, have your car thoroughly cleaned."

Back at the tavern, the three Raiders hugged, careful not to hurt Joe's broken ribs. Billy popped the trunk, and Vince and Joe retrieved their bags; Vince also grabbed the battering ram. When they had their bags in the trunk of their cars, Billy and Joe left for Jacksonville and Atlanta, and Vince headed to his storage unit.

As soon as he got there, he removed his mud-covered boots and clothes and changed back into his civilian garb. Vince checked his watch and saw it was already 7:00 pm. He'd been gone from his mom's house for almost three hours and didn't have time to clean the floor and dispose of the boots and clothes, and that would have to wait until the next day.

Vince made it back to Mt. Pleasant by 7:15 pm and found Shelly and Katy in the den watching TV.

"Well, look who decided to come home," Shelly said and noticed Vince had no shopping bags. "Where are all the clothes you were supposed to buy?"

Vince explained he couldn't decide and wanted to bring Katy to help pick out what he'd need. "She's got better taste than me."

"That's for sure," Katy said. "I'm surprised you didn't get a camouflaged business suit."

Vince smiled. "I'm going to get something to eat. Does anyone need anything?"

Shelly stood and started to the kitchen. "I've got your plate in the fridge. You sit with Katy, and I'll warm it up."

As soon as Shelly left, Vince asked Katy how she was feeling.

"Much better. It's really nice to be with your mom, even if she talks nonstop."

"Don't I know," Vince said. "That's great. I'm sure your car is still at the property you showed the other day. I thought, if you're up to it, we could pick it up in the morning, and you could drive back to your place. I'll follow you."

Katy hesitated before she said, "What about the man that attacked me?"

"I don't think you have to worry about him anymore," Vince replied.

This surprised Katy, and she was about to question him further when Shelly returned to the den with a plate of food.

"Katy, grab that folding table. Our boy needs his nourishment after all those hours of shopping."

Vince finished his meal, and the three of them watched a movie until about 10:00 pm. Shelly said she had a big day and was going to bed. Katy was also ready to get some sleep, and Vince walked her back to her bedroom. Katy shut the door and said, "Okay, what did you mean that I don't have to worry about that man anymore? Hell, Vince, you didn't go to the mall. Did you? What did you do?"

"You're going to have to trust me on this. Just know you'll be safe now from Romano and his people and the man that attacked you."

"What did you do?" Katy persisted, this time with more emotion.

Vince knew he'd have to tell Ryan what he did and said, "I promise I'll tell you everything tomorrow. Have a good sleep, and I'll see you in the morning." Vince left without another word.

Katy wasn't happy but relented because it was clear she'd get nothing more out of him that night.

CHAPTER 28

VINCE WAS UP early for his morning run. When he returned, he found Shelly dressed in the kitchen, having coffee.

"Hey, Mom."

"Hey, yourself."

Vince told Shelly that Katy was feeling much better, and they both agreed she was ready to go back to her apartment. "Don't worry. I'll make sure she gets back safely," he added.

"I also noticed she was more alert yesterday," Shelly said. "I'm going to miss having her around, but I know she'll love getting back to her own place."

"What about me, Mom?"

"I'll miss you too, sweetheart. But now I need to leave for work. Give her a hug from me and tell her we'll talk soon."

Shelly left, and Vince poured himself a cup of coffee. He went to the bedroom to check on Katy. She was still asleep, and he took a seat in the sofa chair next to her bed. He thought of all the terrible things that had happened to her over the last several weeks. But he couldn't help but admit it was nice to be with her again. Despite their differences, he still had deep feelings for her and wished they could have worked it out.

A few minutes later, Katy woke, rolled to her side, and smiled at Vince. "Good morning. What time is it?"

"Almost nine," Vince said. "How are you feeling today?"

"Good," she said but refused to talk about her nightmares.

Vince stood. "I'll get you some coffee."

"Thanks," Katy said. "Give me a few minutes, and I'll come out there."

When she showed up ten minutes later, Vince was seated and pointed to a hot cup of coffee on the kitchen table across from him.

Katy joined him and smiled. "Thanks. That's nice." The smile disappeared. "You didn't go to the mall yesterday, did you? What's going on? You said I don't have to worry anymore."

"I'll tell you everything, but I also owe Ryan an explanation. I'm going to see him tonight, and I'll tell you both everything."

"Tell me now, Vince!"

"Tonight," Vince replied. "Now finish your coffee and go ahead and get dressed and pack your things. I'll take you to get your car."

Katy stared at Vince for a moment and got up and left—her coffee untouched. Vince turned off the coffee maker, emptied and washed both cups, and went to pack his own things.

Thirty minutes later, Vince had his backpack in the VW and was walking back to the house when Katy appeared at the door.

She gave him her suitcase and walked to his car. Vince put Katy's suitcase in the back seat of the VW, and she got in the car.

He turned to Katy. "Are you okay?"

"Yeah, just frustrated. You're so stubborn."

Vince grinned and said, "Well, that makes two of us."

"Just drive," she said, and Vince left for Buckley Lane and Katy's Caprice.

They drove in silence. It took a good half hour to make it to the James Island house. Katy's car keys were still in her briefcase. She retrieved them and got out of the VW without a word.

Vince rolled down his window. "I've got your things. I'll follow you."

By the time Katy made it to Mt. Pleasant, she had cooled down a bit. Vince pulled in and parked next to her. He'd got her suitcase out of the VW and was at her door as she unlocked it.

"Wait here," he said. "Let me check it out." He walked past Katy into the apartment, put down her suitcase, and made sure everything was as it should be. He returned to the door and told Katy she could come in.

"Thanks."

"I'll see you at Ryan's at five, right?" he said.

"Okay," she replied without looking at him.

"Good. Five o'clock then," Vince said, leaving Katy's apartment for his storage unit. He'd packed a trash bag and some towels before leaving Shelly's house. As soon as he got to the unit, it didn't take him long to clean the floor. He put the dirty towels and his muddy boots and pants in the trash bag and left for Ryan's apartment. On the way, Vince found a restaurant that was not yet open. He drove around to the rear of the building and tossed the garbage bag in one of their large trash containers.

It was almost noon by the time he made it to Ryan's duplex. Vince saw the Silverado was gone and, using the key Ryan gave him, unlocked the door, and entered the duplex. He immediately changed into his running shoes and shorts. He felt good, and the miles melted away as he ran through the neighborhoods surrounding Ryan's apartment. Eddie Russo, Michael Coppola, and Frank Romano never entered his mind. Instead, thoughts of Billy Hawk, Joe Knight, and his other Raider brothers began to trickle through his consciousness. He missed them all, but it was time to move on with his life. Vince felt light on his feet and, reaching the five-mile mark, continued running for another few miles before returning to the apartment.

When Vince made it back, he saw Ryan's truck parked in front of the duplex. As soon as he walked into the apartment, Ryan asked him how Katy was doing.

"She's much better. In fact, I took her back to her apartment this morning. She's going to work for a while but wants to do something with us tonight. That is if you're up to it. She's coming over around five o'clock."

"Sounds great."

"What are you up to today?" Vince asked.

"I've got basketball at two this afternoon. Actually, why don't you come? We could always use another guy."

Vince laughed. "I played a little bit overseas, but I'm not in your league. Plus, I just ran eight miles."

"Come on, big guy. What about all those Marine twenty-mile runs you told me about?"

Vince still felt good and thought to himself, *Oh, hell. Why not? I can play a game or two and then watch.* He told Ryan he'd play but needed to take a quick shower and change into a clean shirt and shorts.

Ryan clapped his hands. "Good idea. You're pretty ripe. Make it quick. We need to leave in about twenty minutes."

They arrived at St. Andrews Park at 2:00 pm, and after warming up, they started playing ball. Vince ended up guarding Ryan for the first two games, and Ryan took him to school with his quick moves and precision shooting.

Vince's team lost the second straight game, and he said, "God, I forgot how good you are. I've embarrassed myself enough. I think I'll sit out for a while."

Vince played another few games but spent most of the afternoon on the sidelines watching Ryan and the guys play. He was impressed with the quality of the players, especially the older men who could hold their own against the younger ones.

The games ended around four o'clock, and Ryan said, "If Katy's coming at five, we better get back to the apartment. We could both use a shower and a cold one."

Vince had already cleaned up and was sitting in the living room when there was a knock at the door. He answered it, and Katy waltzed right past him. "Okay, I'm here. Now tell me what you really did yesterday."

"Slow down, Katy. Ryan's finishing getting dressed, and he'll be out here in a minute. I promise I'll tell both of you everything. Can I get you something to drink?"

"Yeah, a beer. I get the feeling I'm going to need one."

Vince grabbed two beers from the fridge, joined Katy in the living room, and handed her one. Nothing was said until Ryan walked out of his bedroom a minute later, his hair wet and wearing no shoes. "Hey, Katy."

"Hi, Ryan," she said without emotion.

Surprised by the way she answered him, Ryan gave Vince a sideways glance.

"Get yourself a beer," Vince said, his tone serious, "I've got something to tell both of you."

Ryan got his beer, returned to the living room, and sat in a chair across from Vince. He leaned forward. "All right, let's have it."

"First of all, Ryan, Katy was attacked a few days ago, and her life threatened."

"Jesus, you told me she fell at work. What's going on?"

Vince nodded towards Katy. "She was attacked while showing a house to what she thought was a client. The person tied her up and said if she testified in the Messina case, he would kill her and the people who worked for her." Vince explained that her wood-be client was actually a man disguised as a woman. "There's no doubt that he was a paid killer hired by Romano."

"God, Katy, are you all right?" Ryan said, his voice filled with concern.

"A little better now, but there's no way I'm testifying."

"That's Katy's choice," Vince said, "and I agree. The problem is that whether Messina is convicted or not, she was never going to be safe as long as they perceived her to be a threat to the Organization. It was my fault Katy got messed up in all this and my responsibility to fix it."

"What did you do, Vince?" Katy asked. "You promised you'd tell me."

"And that's what I'm doing. I first contacted two men I served with in the Raiders and asked them to come to Charleston." He explained how the three of them broke into Romano's office in North Charleston. "One of my men was shot in the chest, but he was wearing a bulletproof vest. Despite a few broken ribs, he'll be okay. Messina was in the office with Romano, and after some hand-to-hand fighting, we finally got both of them under control and tied up."

"Was anyone else hurt?" Ryan asked.

"One of my brothers did a number on Messina, but other than that, nobody was seriously hurt."

"What did you do next?" Katy said.

"I'd learned that Romano has a daughter named Teresa that goes to school at Northwestern up in Chicago. I made it clear that someone would pay her a visit if anything happened to you. Then we discovered something even more effective than that. Romano's computer was open on his desk, showing a spreadsheet containing all the monthly money his organization had taken in. It even showed a breakdown of different categories of criminal activities in all the neighborhoods he controlled. And believe me, it was a lot of money."

Vince explained that if any of them were harmed in any way, a copy of the spreadsheet would be sent to the authorities. And, if that wasn't enough to convince Romano to back off, a copy would be sent to his boss in Chicago. "And he knows what will happen to him if Chicago gets wind the FBI and local police have a copy."

"God, Vince," Ryan interrupted, "I can't believe you did all that."

"I never would have been able to without help from my fellow Raiders."

"Are you sure that's enough to keep us safe?" Katy asked.

"As sure as I can be," Vince said. "Like any father, Romano loves his daughter and wouldn't want any harm to come to her. Also, if he wants to keep his operation in Charleston and stay healthy, he'll make sure the authorities never see that spreadsheet."

"When did all this go down?" Ryan asked.

"Yesterday."

"This whole thing is nuts," Ryan said and held up his empty can. "I'm going to finish getting cleaned up, but I need another one of these before that."

Ryan got another beer, went to his room, and shut the door.

Katy shook her head and smiled. "I can't believe you did all that. I wish there was a way I could thank you. I think you may have just saved my life."

"Well," Vince said, "I guess I was a little selfish. I can't see me getting by without you around, and I wish I hadn't screwed up our marriage."

"I did my part to mess it up, too." Katy got out of her chair and sat next to Vince. She took his hand and said, "I think we should go out tonight. Just the two of us. I can tell you how you screwed up, and you can tell me how I did."

"I'd like that," Vince said, "but what about Ryan?"

Katy smiled. "I think he'll survive one night without us."

It was Vince's turn to smile. "So, is this like a date or what?"

"I don't know," she said, "let's just see where it goes."

Ryan returned to the living room—his hair dried and wearing a pair of Air Jordans. "Everyone ready?"

Vince and Katy stood up—their hands still together.

"We love you, buddy. But I think Katy and I might do this thing together tonight. Is that okay with you?"

Ryan saw them holding hands. "Sure, no problem. Actually, I'm kind of tired from crushing you on the courts today. I guess I'll order another pizza. You two go ahead; I'll be fine."

Vince and Katy walked to the door. "Thanks, buddy," Vince said and slipped his arm around Katy's waist.

"You guys have fun," Ryan said. "I'll see you later."

"We will," Vince replied. "Oh, and don't wait up for us."

Katy gave an impish grin at Vince and said, "Well, soldier boy, when do you ship out?"

"Not going anywhere, ma'am. Except to dinner with you."

Vince and Katy left arm in arm.

After they shut the door, Ryan shook his head, smiled, and said, "Well, here we go again."

ABOUT THE AUTHOR

Geoff Collins holds graduate degrees in business and finance and a master's degree in education. He has held multiple management positions in Fortune 500 companies and was CEO of a Midwest advertising and public relations firm.

After a successful career in business, he taught elementary school for fifteen years. His passion for teaching reading and writing to his students led to a career as an author of both children stories and adult mysteries.

Geoff lives on Johns Island, South Carolina, with his wife, Sally. He has three grown children, Max, Leigh, and KC, and four grandchildren, John, Collin, Cora, and Lily.

OTHER BOOKS BY
GEOFF AND ART COLLINS

NIKKI AND THE TREE KEEPER

"What a wonderful and lovely tale!"

"Nikki is a heart-warming and inspirational story of finding your place in the world."

"Nikki and the Tree Keeper is magical."

"The illustrations are beautiful and add so much to the book."

www.booksbycollins.com

The Christmas Token

"The Christmas Token is a heart-warming holiday tale about generosity, memories, and family."

"The artwork in this tender story is superior!"

"The Christmas Token should become a family tradition to read as the Christmas season begins!"

"Excellent!"

"Lovely book! My kids have read it many times over the holidays."

www.booksbycollins.com

The Adventures of ...
Archibald & Jockabeb

"One of a kind!"

This is the best book EVER!!!!!! Dragons, Indians, horses, evil crows, there is nothing like it! I loved it … can't wait for more adventures to come.

"A majestic tale—*Harry Potter* meets *The Indian in the Cupboard*"

Loved reading these books. I quickly got hooked, dug in, and engaged with the characters. Wonderful stories.

"Rich in vocabulary!"

This book is rich in vocabulary. I can't wait to read all the other Archibald and Jockabeb books!

"Best of the best!"

In the Forest is an outstanding book! The characters are great and help make the wonderful story come together.

"Terrific series of action books!"

www.booksbycollins.com

White Cloud and the Golden Canyon

Excellent Native American tale for children and adults alike.

Wonderful life lessons for all.

Very enjoyable and true to our culture. (Akta Lakota Museum)

www.booksbycollins.com

The Black Creek Mysteries

Alex Foster and Travis Sanders live in a small southern Ohio farm town named Rivers Edge. Their first adventure takes them to the remote desert town of Sunshine, Arizona, where they find themselves in the middle of the Legend of the Apache Death Cave. The following summer, after Alex and Travis graduate from high school, they head to the small fishing town of Black Creek, Maine, for a relaxing vacation before they both head off to college. Their trip becomes anything but relaxing when they discover a mysterious creature in an underwater cave and a network of deadly gunrunners.

www.booksbycollins.com

The Mercy Killings

"Well Written … Interesting Characters and Plenty of Suspense"

Good mystery with interesting characters and plenty of suspense. A cybersecurity expert is hired to determine if narcotics theft is taking place at Charleston SC hospital and who is behind it. Well written with lots of fascinating details.

"Wonderfully Crafted Story Set in Charleston"

Wonderfully crafted story set in Charleston, SC—great story line and vivid imagery. Collins follows Giordano with insight and honesty. Can't wait for Nick's next adventure.

"A Fast and Exciting Read"

The book was a fast read. It was exciting and held my interest throughout. Hope to see more from this author.

www.booksbycollins.com

The Tools of the Trade

Mario Rossini's Jersey syndicate, the Beltran-Lyve Cartel, and the KKK's Confederate White Knights are all battling for control over Charleston's drug trade. Nick Giordano and his friends once again find themselves entangled in the fight. And this time they may all be targets for the legendary Mafia hitman, Carlos Tucci.

"Another Wild Ride"

Tools of the Trade takes us on another wild ride with Nick Giordano and his crew. Collins, as he did with his previous book in this three-part series (volume three is coming in 2019), deftly weaves on intricate story line that builds to a satisfying, thrilling end. Highly recommend Collins, a writer who deserves a vast readership.

"Excitement and Suspense"

Excitement and suspense as mafia and white supremacists fight over the drug market in Charleston SC. Characters well-developed and interesting story line.

www.booksbycollins.com

Shark Bait

Nick Giordano and his friends are drawn into the dark and dangerous world of the Russian mafia. The East Coast Russian mafia boss, Dimitri "The Shark" Pavlov, and his enforcer, Viktor Dudko, are using Charleston's Port Authority terminals for drug smuggling and human trafficking.

"Hopefully More to Come"

In this series, which sadly wraps here with Book Three, Collins found a higher gear with each, serving up a fresh batch of nasty folks for the series' core characters to root out and take down. That the books were set in Charleston only added to their delight. The only rotten aspect here is that this is the last we'll see of Nick Giordano and his pals—that is, unless, this crew comes around for cameos in one of Collins' future works. Hats off!

www.booksbycollins.com

A Death in the Family

Detective Adam Stone and his partner, Marcus Williams, are part of Charleston's elite Organized Crime Unit investigating a spike in the city's heroin and fentanyl drug trade. During a raid of a major drug distribution house, the shot-caller of the Bloods is shot and killed by Adam. Shortly after that, his wife, Ann, is found murdered. Initially, the Bloods are the obvious suspects. However, as the story unfolds, several other women are murdered, and the list of possible suspects grows. It soon becomes apparent that there is a serial killer roaming the street of Charleston.

www.booksbycollins.com

Prime Suspects

Prime Suspects is the second in the Adam Stone action-packed murder/mystery series. The dead body of the Joe Wallace, one of Charleston's premier defense attorneys, has just washed up on the shores of the Ashley River. Wallace possessed a dubious reputation as a heavy drinker, gambler, and frequent user of various controlled substances—not to mention his notoriety for chasing skirt. There are no shortage of suspects, and as Adam Stone moves deeper into the investigation, the list continues to grow. One by one, he eliminates the potential killers until he finds himself face to face with the most dangerous of them all … the prime suspect.

www.booksbycollins.com

The Sandman

In the third book of the Adam Stone detective series, Adam and his partner, Marcus Williams, investigate the late-night murder of a Charleston physical therapist. Soon two other therapists are murdered, and the detectives find themselves embroiled in the middle of an international Chinese opioid smuggling operation. The case eventually leads to the discovery of a connection between the Chinese Triad and the Chicago mafia. The possibility of additional murders rise as word on the street hints that an old mysterious mafia hitman has arrived in Charleston. Adam and Marcus know that they will now come face to face with the legend of the one of the world's most deadly assassin— the Sandman.

www.booksbycollins.com

A Dangerous Game

Minor league pitcher, Joe Nash, learns of his estranged father's unexpected death. He returns to Charleston, South Carolina, only to find his accountant father had for years been working for low-level gangsters funneling dirty money to an offshore account in the Cayman Islands. To make amends for his failure as a parent, Joe's father transfers the funds into a secret bank account in Belize and leaves a series of clues leading Joe and his sister, Emily, to find the multimillion-dollar treasure. However, Joe and his sister learn they are not the only ones searching for money, and it soon becomes a race not only to find the money but also to save their lives!

www.booksbycollins.com

Reading Partners is a nonprofit literacy organization that re-cruits and trains community volunteers to provide one-on-one reading tutoring to students in under-resourced schools across the country. This highly effective program has helped thousands of children master the fundamental reading skills they need to succeed in school and beyond. For more information, please visit www.readingpartners.org.

"Literacy is not a luxury; it is a right and a responsibility. If our world is to meet the challenges of the twenty-first century we must harness the energy and creativity of all our citizens."

–President Bill Clinton